ALSO BY BOBBIE ANN MASON

FICTION

Shiloh and Other Stories
In Country
Spence + Lila
Love Life
Feather Crowns
Midnight Magic

NONFICTION

The Girl Sleuth
Nabokov's Garden
Clear Springs

ZIGZAGGING DOWN A WILD TRAIL

Bobbie Ann Mason

ZIGZAGGING
DOWN A
WILD TRAIL

◆ STORIES

RANDOM HOUSE

NEW YORK

Copyright © 2001 by Bobbie Ann Mason

All rights reserved under International and Pan-American Copyright Conventions. Published in the United States by Random House, Inc., New York, and simultaneously in Canada by Random House of Canada Limited, Toronto.

RANDOM HOUSE and colophon are registered trademarks of Random House, Inc.

The following stories have been previously published: "With Jazz" appeared in the February 26, 1990, issue of *The New Yorker;* "Thunder Snow" appeared in the Spring 1997 issue of *DoubleTake;* "Rolling into Atlanta" appeared in the Winter 1992 issue of *Ploughshares;* "The Funeral Side" appeared in the Summer 1999 issue of *The Southern Review;* "Tobrah" appeared in the Summer 1990 issue of *Story;* "Proper Gypsies" appeared in *The Southern Review,* 1995; "Charger" appeared in the January 1998 issue of *The Atlantic;* "Three-Wheeler" appeared in the June 2001 issue of *The Atlantic;* and "Window Lights" appeared in the Autumn 1997 issue of *Story.*

Grateful acknowledgment is made to the following for permission to reprint previously published material:

HAL LEONARD CORPORATION: Excerpt from "Ole Buttermilk Sky" from the motion picture *Canyon Passage,* words and music by Hoagy Carmichael and Jack Brooks. Copyright © 1946 by Morley Music Co. Copyright renewed by Morley Music Co. and Frank Music Corp. Excerpt from "England Swings", words and music by Roger Miller. Copyright © 1963 by Sony/ATV Songs LLC. Copyright renewed. All rights administered by Sony/ATV Music Publishing, 8 Music Square West, Nashville, TN, 37203. International copyright secured. All rights reserved. Used by permission.

JON LANDAU MANAGEMENT: Excerpt from "Hungry Heart" by Bruce Springsteen. Copyright © 1980 by Bruce Springsteen (ASCAP). Reprinted by permission of Jon Landau Management. The author extends special thanks to Bruce Springsteen for the use of his lyric "I took a wrong turn and I just kept going."

Library of Congress Cataloging-in-Publication Data
Mason, Bobbie Ann.
Zigzagging down a wild trail: stories/Bobbie Ann Mason.
p. cm.
ISBN 0-679-44924-8
1. United States—Social life and customs—20th century—Fiction.
I. Title.
PS3563.A7877 Z35 2001
813'.54—dc21   00-066480
Printed in the United States of America on acid-free paper
Random House website address: www.atrandom.com

9 8 7 6 5 4 3 2

First Edition

Book design by Victoria Wong

For Roger

Contents

ZIGZAGGING
DOWN A
WILD TRAIL

◆ ◆ ◆

With Jazz

I never paid much attention to current events, all the trouble
in the world you hear about. I was too busy raising a family.
But my children have all gone now and I've started to think
about things that go on. Why would my daughter live with a
man and get ready to raise a baby and refuse to marry the
guy? Why would my son live in a cabin by the river and not
see a soul for months on end? But that's just personal. I'm
thinking of the bigger picture, too. It seems a person barely
lives long enough to begin to see where his little piece fits in
the universal puzzle. I'm not old but I imagine that old people start to figure out how to live just when it's too late.

These thoughts come up at my weekly neighborhood
group. It started out as a weight-reducing club, but we kept
meeting even after we all got skinny. Now on Fridays after
work a bunch of us get together at somebody's house and

talk about life, in a sort of talk-show format. Although we laugh a lot, for us it's survival. And it helps me think.

It's so hard to be nice to people. It's something you have to learn. I try to be nice, but it's complicated. You start feeling guilty for your own failures of generosity at just about the same point in life when you start feeling angry, even less willing to give. The two feelings collide—feeling gracious and feeling mean. When you get really old, they say, you go right back to being a child, spiteful and selfish, and you don't give a damn what people think. In between childhood and old age, you have this bubble of consciousness—and conscience. It's enough to drive you crazy.

After our group session last Friday, I went up to Paducah, across the county line, hoping to see this guy I know. He calls himself Jazz, but his real name is Peter. He always hated that name. Kids in school would tease him. "Where's your peter?," "Oh, you don't look like a peter," etc. Some kids from my distant past used the word "goober," the first name I ever heard for the secret male anatomy. I thought they were saying "cooper." That didn't make any sense to me. Then I learned that the correct word was "goober." I learned that in the fourth grade from Donna Lee Washam, the day she led me on an expedition to a black-walnut tree on the far edge of the playground. She came back to the classroom with two black walnuts in her panties and giggled all afternoon as she squirmed in her seat. Across the aisle and a couple of seats up, Jerry Ray Baxter sometimes took his goober out and played with it. He couldn't talk plain, and after that year he stopped coming to school.

Jazz was at the Top Line, where I thought he'd be. He was lounging at the bar, with a draught beer, shooting the breeze. When he saw me he grinned slowly and pulled a new brassiere out of his pocket, dangling it right there between the jug of beet-pickled eggs and the jug of pickled pigs' feet.

Ed, the bartender, swung his head like he'd seen it all. "There you go again, Jazz, pulling off women's clothes." Jazz said, "No, this is my magic trick." I stuffed the bra in my purse. "Thanks, Jazz. I guess you knew my boobs were falling down."

He came from down in Obion, Tennessee, and grew up duck hunting around Reelfoot Lake. Now he goes to France and brings back suitcases full of French underwear. He sells it to a boutique and occasionally to friends. It's designer stuff and the sizes are different from here. His ex-wife gets it at cost from a supplier in Paris where she works. He goes over there once a year or so to see his kids. Jazz works construction and saves his money, and then he quits and lights out for France. I've got a drawerful of expensive bras he's given me—snap-fronts, plunges, crisscrosses, strapless—all in lace and satin.

"That's a special number," he said, moving close to me. "Scalloped lace and satin stretch. Molded cup, underwire. I'll want to check the fitting later."

I grinned. "We'll see about that, Jazz. Tonight I feel like getting drunk."

"You're gonna be a granny again in a few months, Chrissy. Is that how an old granny's supposed to act?" he teased.

"But I'm happy, damn it! I feel like I'm in love."

"One of these days I'll make you fall in love with me, Chrissy."

I ordered a bourbon. What Jazz needed, I thought, was a woman who felt romantic about him. But he'd never make a claim on a woman he cared about. He'd always step aside and let the woman go fall in love with some clod who jerked her around.

Glancing up at a TV newsbreak—a local update on water pollution—I said, "All the mussels in the lake are dying. It's all those pesticides."

"I heard it was last year's drought," said Jazz. "That's natural."

"Here I am celebrating a new baby coming into the world—for what? To see a dead lake? And air not fit to breathe?"

Jazz touched my shoulder, to steady me. "World's always had trouble. No baby ever set foot in the Garden of Eden."

I laughed. "That's just like you to say that, Jazz."

"You think you know me, don't you?" he said.

"I know you well enough to feel sorry I always treat you so bad."

Ed set my drink before me and I took it eagerly. I said to Jazz, "Why don't you ever get mad at me, tell me off?"

He punched my arm, buddy style. "You should never go away mad at a person, because one of you might get killed on the way home."

The regular crowd was there at the Top Line—good old boys who worked at the plants, guys wandering around loose on a Friday night while their wives took the kids to the mall. A tall man entering the bar caught my eye. He walked like he had money. He had on an iridescent-green shirt, with a subtle paisley design that made my eyes tingle. His pants had cowboy-style piping on the pocket plackets. Over the shirt he wore a suède vest with fuchsia embroidery and zippered pockets.

"That's Buck Joiner, the radio guy," Jazz said, reading my mind.

Buck Joiner was the D.J. I listened to while I was getting ready for work. His "Morning Mania" show was a roaring streak of pranks and risqué jokes and call-in giveaways. Once, he actually telephoned Colonel Qaddafi in Libya. He got through to the palace and talked to some official who spoke precise English with a Middle Eastern accent.

As soon as I felt I'd had enough bourbon, I marched over to Buck Joiner's table, wielding my glass.

"I listen to you," I said. "I've got your number on my dial."

He seemed bored. It was like meeting Bob Dylan or some big shot you know won't be friendly.

"I called you up once," I went on recklessly. "You were giving away tickets to the Ray Stevens show. I was trying to be the twenty-fifth caller. But my timing wasn't right."

"Too bad," he said, deadpan. He was with a couple of guys in suits. Blanks.

"I've got to work on my timing." I paused, scrambling for contact. "You should interview my Friday-afternoon talk group."

"What's that?"

"We're a group of ladies. We get together every Friday and talk about life."

"What about life?" Out of the side of his face, he smirked for the benefit of the suits.

"The way things are going. Stuff." My mind went blank. I knew there was more to it than that. Right then, I really wanted him to interview our group. I knew we sparkled with life and intelligence. Rita had her opinions on day care, and Dorothy could rip into the abortion issue, and Phyllis believed that psychiatrists were witch doctors. Me, I could do my Bette Davis imitations.

"Here's my card," I said, whipping one out of my purse. I'd ordered these about a month ago, just for the privilege of saying that.

"It's nice to meet a fan," he said with stretched lips—not a true smile.

"Don't give me that, buddy. If it weren't for your listeners, you wouldn't be sitting here with all that fancy piping scrawled all over you."

I rejoined Jazz, who had been watching out for me. "I'd like to see Oprah nail him to the wall," I said to Jazz.

Of course, I was embarrassed. That was the trouble. I was lost somewhere between being nice and being mean. I shouldn't drink. I don't know why I was so hard on the D.J., but he was a man I had depended on to start my day, and he turned out to be a shit. From now on I'd listen to his show and think, Stuck-up turdface. Yet there I was in a French bra and with an unusual amount of cleavage for this area. I didn't know what I was getting at. Jazz was smiling, touching my hand, ordering me another drink. Jazz wore patience like adhesive tape.

In bits and pieces, I've told this at the Friday talk group: My first husband, Jim Ed, was my high-school boyfriend. We married when we were seniors, and they didn't let me graduate, because I was pregnant. I used to say that I barely understood how those things worked, but that was a lie. Too often I exaggerate my innocence, as if trying to excuse myself for some of the messes I've gotten myself into. Looking back now, I see that I latched on to Jim Ed because I was afraid there'd never be another opportunity in my life, and he was the best of the pickings around there. That's the way I do everything. I grab anything that looks like a good chance, right then and there. I even tend to overeat, as if I'm afraid I won't ever get another good meal. "That's the farm girl in you," my second husband, George, always said. He was an analytical person and had a theory about everything. When he talked about the Depression mentality of our parents' generation he made it sound physically disgusting. He had been to college. I never did go back and get my high-school diploma, but that's something I'm thinking about doing now. George couldn't just enjoy something for what it was. We'd grill steaks and he'd come up with some reason why we

were grilling steaks. He said it went back to caveman behavior. He said we were acting out an ancient scene. He
made me feel trapped in history, as though we hadn't ad-
vanced since cavemen. I don't guess people have changed
that much, though, really. I bet back in caveman times there
was some know-it-all who made his woman feel dumb.
After a while, I didn't pay any attention to George, but
then my little daughter died. She had meningitis, and it was
fairly sudden and horrible. I was still in shock a month later,
when George started nagging at me about proper grief dis-
plays and the stages of grief. I blew up. I told him to walk.
What we really should have done was share the grief. I'm
sure the most basic textbook would say that. But instead he's
lecturing me on my grief. You can't live with somebody who
lectures you on your grief. I'll have my grief in peace, I told
him. Kathy wasn't his daughter. He couldn't possibly know
how I felt. That was so long ago he doesn't seem real to me.
He still lives around here. I've heard that he married again
and that he raises rabbits and lives out in the country, out
near Bardwell—none of which I would have ever imagined.
But, you know, as small as this place is, I've never laid eyes on
him again. Maybe he's changed so much I just don't recognize him when I see him.

"How did you just happen to have that bra in your pocket,
Jazz?" I wanted to know, but he only grinned. It was like carrying around condoms in case of emergency, I thought. The
bra was just my size. I'd put it on in the restroom. The one I
had worn was stretching out, and I left it in the trash can. Let
people wonder.

At first, I thought Kathy just had the flu. She had a fever
and she said her head was splitting—a remark so calm that
she might have said her hands were dirty in the same tone. It
was summer, a strange time for flu, so I hurried all the kids

on out to their grandmother's that Sunday, like always, thinking the country air would make Kathy feel better. Don and Phil kept aggravating her because she didn't want to play in Mama's attic or go out to the barn. She lay around under one of Mama's quilts, and I thought later, with a hideous realization, that she somehow knew she was going to die. You never know what a child is thinking, or how scared they might be, or how they've blown something up in their imagination. She was twelve, and she'd just started her period a couple of months before. I thought her sickness might be related to that. The doctor just laughed at me when I brought that up. Can you imagine the nerve? It's only now that I've gotten mad about that. But I hear that that doctor has had a stroke and is in a nursing home. What good do bad feelings do when so much time has passed? That's what Jazz says.

George blamed me for taking her out to Mama's that day. He was gone to an engineering convention in Nashville; he was a chemical engineer at Carbide then. He said there was no reason a child shouldn't recover from meningitis. He wagged a book in my face, but I refused to read what he had found on the disease. I thought it would kill me to know her death was my fault. I guess George wasn't such a bad guy. He just had his ways. I think we all do and none of us knows how to be sensitive enough, it seems. He probably just didn't know how to deal with the situation. It occurred to me recently that maybe he felt guilty for being away at the time, just as I felt guilty for not noticing how quiet and withdrawn she was, as though she was figuring it all out for herself. Kathy was in 4-H, and that year she was working on a Holly Hobbie display for the fair—the little girl hiding her face in the calico bonnet. Kathy sewed the clothes herself, and she was making a little stuffed dog and decorating a flower basket for the scene. I still have that unfinished Holly Hobbie scene—in the closet in a stereo box. I should probably get rid of it, because if Kathy had lived she would have grown out of that phase, but all I have is those little scraps of the way Kathy was, the only reality she ever had.

Don and Phil grew up and left as soon as they got cars. Can you believe anybody would name their sons after the Everly Brothers? I reckon I'd still do something that silly. But I never told them we named them for the Everly Brothers. Jim Ed, the father of all my children, loved the Everly Brothers, and he used to play them in his truck, back when eight-track tape decks were a new thing. Jim Ed was loose about a lot of things, and he never criticized me the way George did. I don't know if he blamed me about Kathy. I have a feeling that if we'd stuck it out we could have learned to love each other better. But he was restless, and he couldn't hang around when we needed him most. He moved over to Cairo and worked on the riverboats—still does. I guess he has some kind of life. The boys see him. Don's wife ran off with one of the riverboat guys and Don lives in a cabin over there. I don't see him very much. He brought me a giant catfish, a mud cat, on Mother's Day. Catfish that big aren't really good to eat, though. He sets trotlines and just lives in the wilderness. I doubt if he'll ever marry again. Phil is the only one of my children who turned out normal. Now, what is there to say about that? A wife with a tortilla face and bad taste in clothes, spoiled kids, living room decorated with brass geese and fish. I go there and my skin breaks out. There's no pleasing me, I guess.

Last week, Laura—my other daughter, the baby—wrote me that she was pregnant. She's barely divorced from this museum director she met at school—he restored old pieces of pottery, glued them together. He made a good living but she wasn't satisfied. Now she's going to be tied down with a baby and a man, this Nick, who does seasonal work of some sort. They're living in his home town, a little place in Arizona, in the desert. I can't imagine what would grow there.

Laura, on the telephone this past Sunday, said, "I don't want to get married again. I don't trust it anymore. And I want to be free of all that bureaucratic crap. I trust Nick more than I trust the government."

"You need the legal protection," I said. "What if something happened to him? What if he ran off and left you? I can tell you exactly how that works."

"I'd have to murder Nick to get him out of my life! Honestly, he's being so devoted it's unbelievable."

"I guess that's why I don't believe it."

"Come on, Mom. Just think, you're going to be a grandma again! Aren't you going to come out when the baby's born? Isn't that what mothers do?"

Laura was five when Kathy died. We didn't take her to the funeral. We told her Kathy had gone off to live with Holly Hobbie in New York. If I could undo that lie, I would. It was worse when she found out the truth, because she was old enough then to understand and the shock hurt her more. I thought my heart would break when I saw Jim Ed at the funeral. I saw him alone only once, for a few minutes in the corridor before the service started, but we couldn't speak what we felt. Jim Ed was crying, and I wanted to cling to him, but we could see George in the other room, standing beside a floral display—a stranger.

Jazz said, "Ever notice how at night it's scary because you feel like your secrets are all exposed, but you trick yourself into thinking they're safe in the dark? Smoky bars, candlelight—that's what all that atmosphere shit is about."

"That's what I always say," I said, a little sarcastically. Sometimes Jazz seemed to be fishing around for something to say and then just making something up to sound deep.

We were driving to see my son Don out at his cabin by the river. It was Jazz's idea, a crazy notion that seized him. He said he felt like driving. He said I needed some air. He didn't let me finish my last drink.

I met Jazz a year ago, in traffic court. We'd both been in minor fender benders on the same road on the same day, at different times. We'd both failed to yield. I remember Jazz saying to me, "I hope that's not a reflection on my character. Normally, I'm a very yielding guy." That day Jazz had on a plaid flannel shirt and boot-flared jeans and a cowboy hat—the usual garb for a man around here. But it was his boots I loved. Pointy-toed, deep-maroon, with insets of Elvis's photograph just above the ankles. He'd found the boots in France. That night we went out for barbecue and he gave me some peach-blush panties with a black lace overlay. We had been friends since then, but we never seemed to get serious. I thought he had a big block of fear inside him.

The cab of his truck was stuffy, that peculiar oil-and-dust smell of every man's truck I've ever been in. I lowered the window and felt the mellow river breeze. Jazz chattered non-stop until we got deep into the country. Then he seemed to hush, as though we were entering a grand old church.

We were traveling on a state road, its winding curves settled comfortably through the bottomland, with its swampy and piney smells. There were no houses, no lights. Now and then we passed an area where kudzu made the telephone poles and bushes look as though they were a giant's furniture covered up with protective sheets. At a stop sign I told Jazz to go straight instead of following the main road. Soon there was a turnoff, unmarked except for an old sign for a church that I knew had burned down in the fifties. We saw an abandoned pickup straddling the ditch. When the road turned to gravel, I counted the turnoffs, looking for the fourth one. Jazz shifted gears and we chugged up a little hill.

"Reckon why he lives way off out here?" Jazz said as he braked and shut off the engine. There were no lights at the cabin, and Don's motorbike was gone. Jazz went over into the bushes for a minute. It was a half-moon night, the kind of night that made you see things in the silhouettes. I thought I saw Don standing by the side of the cabin, peering around the corner, watching us.

Jazz reached through the truck's open window and honked the horn.

I heard an owl answer the horn. When I was little I thought owls were messengers from the preachers in charge of Judgment Day. "Who will be the ones?" I remember our preacher saying. "Who?" Even then I pictured Judgment Day as an orchestrated extravaganza, like a telethon or a musical salute. I never took religion seriously. I'm glad I didn't force my children into its frightful clutches. But maybe that was the trouble, after all.

We stood on the sagging porch, loaded with fishnets and crates of empties—Coke and beer bottles. The lights from the pickup reflected Jazz and me against the cabin windows. I tried the door, and it opened into the kitchen.

"Don?" I called.

I found the kitchen light, just a bulb and string. The cord was new. It still had that starched feel, and the little metal bell on the end knot was shiny and sharp. It made me think of our old bathroom light when Jim Ed and I first married. It was the first thing I'd touch in the morning when I'd get up and rush to the bathroom to throw up.

The table was set for one, with the plate turned face over and the glass upside down. Another glass contained an assortment of silverware. A little tray held grape jelly and sugar and instant coffee and an upside-down mug.

The cabin was just one room, and the daybed was neatly made, spread with one of my old quilts. I sat down on the bed. I felt strange, as though all my life I had been zigzagging down a wild trail to this particular place. I stared at the familiar pattern of the quilt, the scraps of the girls' dresses and the boys' shirts. Kathy had pieced some of the squares. If I looked hard, I could probably pick out some of her childish stitches.

"This is weird," said Jazz. He was studying some animal bones spread out on a long table fashioned from a door. "What do you reckon he's aiming to do with these?"

"He always liked biology," I said, rising from the bed. I smoothed and straightened the quilt, thinking about Goldilocks trespassing at the three bears' house.

The table was littered: bones, small tools, artist's brushes and pens, a coffee cup with a drowned cigarette stub, more butts nesting in an upturned turtle shell, some bright foil paper, an oily rag. Jazz flipped through a tablet of drawings of fangs and fishbones.

"He must be taking a summer course at the community college," I said, surprised. "He talked about that back in the spring, but I didn't believe it."

"Look at these," Jazz said. "They're good. How can anybody do that?" he said in amazement.

We studied the drawings. In the careful, exact lines I saw faint glimpses of my young child, and his splashy crayon pictures of monsters taped to the kitchen wall. Seeing his efforts suddenly mature was like running into a person I recognized but couldn't place. Most of the pictures were close-ups of bones, but some were sketches of fish and birds. I liked those better. They had life to them. Eagerly, I raced through two dozen versions of a catfish. The fish was long and slim, like a torpedo. Its whiskers curved menacingly, and its body was accurately mottled. It even looked slippery. I stared at the catfish, almost as if I expected it to speak.

I jerked a blank sheet of paper from the tablet of drawings and worked on a note:

Dear Don,

It's 10:30 P.M. Friday and I came out here with a friend to see if you were home. We just dropped by to say hello. Please let me know how you are. Nothing's wrong. I've got some good news. And I'd love to see you.

Love,
Mom

"It doesn't sound demanding, does it?" I asked as Jazz read it.

"No, not at all."

"It almost sounds like one of those messages on an answering machine—stilted and phony."

Jazz held me as if he thought I might cry. I wasn't crying. He held my shoulders till he was sure I'd got the tears back in and then we left. I couldn't say why I wasn't crying. But nothing bad had happened. There wasn't anything tragic going on. My daughter was having a baby—that was the good news. My son had drawn some fishbones—drawings that were as fine as lace.

"Me and my bright ideas," Jazz said apologetically.

"It's O.K., Jazz. I'll track Don down some other time."

As we pulled out, Jazz said, "The wilderness makes me want to go out in it. I've got an idea. Tomorrow let's go for a long hike on one of those trails up in Shawnee National Forest. We can take backpacks and everything. Let's explore caves! Let's look for bears and stuff!"

I laughed. "You could be Daniel Boone and I could be Rebecca."

"I don't think Rebecca went for hikes. You'll have to be some Indian maiden Daniel picked up."

"Did Daniel Boone really do that sort of thing?" I said, pretending to be scandalized.

"He was a true explorer, wasn't he?" Jazz said, hitting the brights just as a deer seemed to drift across the road.

Jazz thought he was trying to cheer me up, but I was already so full of joy I couldn't even manage to tell him. I let him go on. He was sexiest when he worked on cheering me up.

It was late, and I wound up at Jazz's place, a sprawling apartment with a speaker system wired into every room. His dog, Butch, met us at the door. While Jazz took Butch out for a midnight stroll, I snooped around. I found a beer in the refrigerator. I had trouble with the top and beer spewed all over Jazz's dinette. When he returned, I started teasing him about all the women's underwear he owned.

"Put some of it on," I urged.

"Are you nuts?"

"Just put it on, for me. I won't tell. Just for fun."

I kept teasing him, and he gave in. We couldn't find any garments that would fit. We hooked two bras together and rigged up a halter. With his lime-green bikini briefs—his own—he looked great, like a guy in a sex magazine. It's surprising what men really wear underneath. I searched for some music to play on Jazz's fancy sound system. I looked for the Everly Brothers but couldn't find them, so I put on a George Winston CD. To be nice, I never said a word about Jazz's taste in music. Exhilarated, I sailed from room to room, following the sound, imagining it was "Let It Be Me" instead. I suddenly felt an overwhelming longing to see Jim

Ed again. I wanted to tell him about Don going to school, drawing pictures, making contact with the world again. I wanted to see the traces of Don's face in his. I wanted the two of us to go out to Arizona and see Laura and the baby when it came. We could make a family photo—Jim Ed and me and Laura, with the baby. The baby's father didn't enter into the vision.

It occurred to me that it takes so long to know another person. No wonder you can run through several, like trying on clothes that don't fit. There are so many to choose from, after all, but when I married Jim Ed it was like an impulse buy, buying the first thing you see. And yet I've learned to trust my intuition on that. Jim Ed was the right one all along, I thought recklessly. And I wasn't ever nice to Jim Ed. I was too young then to put myself in another person's place. Call it ignorance of the imagination. Back then I had looked down on him for being country, for eating with his arms anchored on the table and for wiping his mouth with the back of his hand. I'd get mad at him for just being himself at times when I thought he should act civilized. Now I've learned you can't change men, and sometimes those airs I'd looked for turn out to be so phony. Guys like Jim Ed always seemed to just be themselves, regardless of the situation. That's why I still loved him, I decided, as I realized I was staring at Jazz's reflection in the mirror—the lime green against the shimmering gold of his skin and the blips of the track lighting above.

Jazz followed me into the bedroom, where we worked at getting rid of our French togs. I was aware that Jazz was talking, aware that he was aware that I might not be listening closely. It was like hearing a story at my little neighborhood talk show. He was saying, "In France, there's this street, rue du Bac. They call streets *rues*. The last time I left Monique and the two kids, it was on that street, a crowded shopping street. The people over there are all pretty small compared to us, and they have this blue-black hair and deep dark eyes and real light skin, like a hen's egg. I waved good-bye and the three of them just blended right into that crowd and disappeared. That's where they belong, and so I'm here. I guess you might say I just couldn't *parlez-vous.*"

"Take me to France, Jazz. We could have a great time."

"Sure, babe. In the morning." Jazz turned toward me and smoothed the cover over my shoulders.

"I love you," Jazz said.

When I woke up at daylight, Jazz was still holding me, curled around me like a mother protecting her baby. The music was still playing, on infinite repeat.

Tobrah

Jackie Holmes had taken two trips by airplane. The first, in 1980, from Kentucky to California, included dinner—a choice between short ribs and cannelloni. Jackie ordered cannelloni because she didn't know what it was. Floating up there above the clouds seemed so unreal—as a child she had imagined God lived there. In Los Angeles, her cousin took her to Disneyland, the stars' homes, and Universal Studios. They drove down Sunset Boulevard, where the palm trees were tall and majestic. Jackie felt privileged, as if all her life, until then, she had never been allowed anything grand.

The second trip, to Oklahoma, not long ago, was different. In Tulsa, Jackie arranged her father's funeral. She hadn't heard from him in more than thirty-five years, since her parents divorced and he left for the West. She hardly recognized the man lying in the casket. Her father's eyes had been his most memorable feature—dark and deep-set, like her own. But now his eyes were shut, impervious to her questions. The mourners, men he had worked with at a meatpacking plant, didn't tell her much. Joe had been drinking, and his pickup slid down an embankment. No one seemed surprised. He left no money or possessions of worth. She brought home a tattered Army blanket she remembered from her childhood and had not thought of since.

But there was something else. Her father had left a child. The little girl was being cared for by a neighbor, a woman with three children of her own. She told Jackie that the child's mother had died the year before and that Joe had been despondent. He left a will naming Jackie as god-parent. Miraculously, after some red tape in a rose-brick court building, Jackie left Oklahoma with the child. Jackie was forty-four and her half sister was almost five. Jackie, long accustomed to the disappointment of having no children of her own, realized that children scared her a little. She felt like a kidnapper.

Tobrah, the child, had not been taken to the funeral, and she didn't seem curious about where her father was. On the airplane, escaping Jackie's questions, she zipped up and down the aisle, talking to passengers. Jackie wasn't used to a child's random energy—the way she squirmed and bounced in the seat, her hands and body busy but her manner oblivi-ous. In the dark apartment that Jackie had cleaned out, she found only a few possessions of Tobrah's—some small toys, a doll and a teddy bear, several T-shirts and pairs of shorts.

"Aren't you cold?" Jackie asked, as she reached up to swivel the air stream away.

"No."

"When we get home I'll buy you some jeans," Jackie said. "And a sweatshirt. What's your favorite color?"

"Green."

"Green? Mine's blue."

"I don't like blue."

When Tobrah dropped off to sleep, Jackie located a blanket in the overhead compartment and draped it over the little girl. The Army blanket was in Jackie's suitcase, tucked away in the plane's belly. The airline blanket was bright blue and made of some kind of foamy synthetic material. Outside, the clouds billowed like a bubble bath.

"What makes you think you can afford to bring up a kid?" Jackie's mother asked when Jackie brought Tobrah to meet her. Tobrah was on the back porch playing with Lorraine's mop-like lap dog. Lorraine lived in a small wood-frame house in an old section of town.

Jackie ignored the question. Her mother had the same attitude about anything—a new car, an appliance, even splurging on a night out. She had a gallon jug full of coins.

"Do you reckon that hair's bleached?" Lorraine asked.

"We'll just have to wait and see," Jackie said impatiently.

Tobrah had a dark complexion, and her hair was a short, tight mass of light curls, darker at the roots. Her eyes were topaz, and her new green T-shirt made flecks of green sparkle in them.

"That name sounds foreign," said Lorraine.

She kept tapping her cigarette in a crowded ashtray. Her gray laminated table had cigarette burns on it. The walls were yellowed from gas-furnace fumes. Jackie's mother had let her place go since she retired from work. She had been a floor-lady for thirty years, and now all she wanted to do was sit. She got on Jackie's nerves.

Tobrah crashed through the door, the dog yapping excitedly at her heels. She demanded a drink of water, and as she gulped from the glass Jackie gave her, she continued to play with the dog—nudging and poking, twisting her body, giggling.

"Honey, tell me something," said Lorraine, hugging Tobrah. "Where did you get that name of yours? Did your mama give it to you?"

"From a story," she said, holding the glass up for Jackie to take.

"Does it mean something?"

Tobrah wriggled out of Lorraine's grasp and grabbed a ragged piece of chewed rawhide from the floor.

"Do you want us to call you Toby?" Lorraine asked.

"No." Tobrah pulled at her hair. She scooped up the dog and went out the back door again.

"Well!" said Lorraine, with a sigh of smoke. "What do you make of that?"

"She won't talk about her mother—or about Daddy either," Jackie said. "I already tried."

Tobrah had told Jackie she didn't remember her mother. She said her father was away on a long trip. He might not be back, she said.

It was true that Jackie couldn't afford to spend much on a child, but it seemed to her that nowadays children had too much. Her California cousin's children had a room full of expensive stuffed animals that they never played with. Jackie's house was a modest brick ranch dating back to her second marriage. She cleared out her sewing room for Tobrah. Jackie's uncle and aunt let her have an old twin bed they weren't using, and at yard sales she found toys and furnishings. She collected hand-me-down clothing from friends. Baby talk didn't come naturally to Jackie, and she stood around awkwardly at store counters and in checkout lines while people burbled enthusiastically to the little girl, as though she were a pet on a leash. They actually said she looked good enough to eat. Being seen with Tobrah, Jackie began to feel an unfamiliar pride. People asked the typical questions: "Whose little girl are you?" and "How old are you?" and "What grade are you in?" Jackie, who was guilty of asking kids the same kinds of questions, had never before realized how trite they were. Yet they were real and important questions. Whose little girl are you? she wanted to know. Where did you get that hair?

Sometimes in the night, Jackie heard Tobrah stirring and thought of prowlers, then remembered. One night she awoke to find Tobrah curled close to her. The child had waited until Jackie had gone to sleep before crawling in with her, as if she didn't want to reveal her need. There was so much Jackie wanted to know. What did Tobrah's mother look like? Did her father love Tobrah? Did he buy her Christmas presents, play dolls with her? When Jackie was small, about Tobrah's age, her father came home once after a weekend trip to Tennessee. She had waited eagerly all day, and when she was exhausted with the excitement of waiting, he finally appeared. He had forgotten to bring her a present. He had promised to bring her a souvenir with the name "Tennessee" written on it. When eventually he left for good, she was glad. Her mother encouraged her to forget him.

Jackie pieced together a few facts about Tobrah. She couldn't read. She had never been to preschool but had been to some kind of day-care facility, a large place where hundreds of children lined up for ice-cream bars in the afternoons. They napped on mats. The woman in charge had "fuzzy hair, big glass eyes, and a fat butt," according to Tobrah.

"Do you miss going there?" Jackie asked one morning a few days after their return from Oklahoma. Jackie was getting ready for work—her bereavement leave was over. Bereavement was a joke, she kept thinking.

Tobrah kicked her feet against the kitchen-chair rungs. She was eating cereal straight from the box. "It smelled like bad soap."

"I have a surprise," Jackie said. "I have a place for you to go while I'm at work. It'll be nicer than that place in Oklahoma."

"I don't want to go."

"Yes, you do. It'll be fun."

"They won't say my name right."

"Well, people around here have a different accent from Oklahoma. They don't always pronounce things right. You'll have to be patient."

Tobrah disappeared into her room. When Jackie went to get her, she found that the child had made up her bed like a polite guest and placed her doll and bear on the pillow. The bedspread was crooked though, and the sheet trailed to the floor.

"Don't you move till I get back," Tobrah said to the toys.

When Jackie left Tobrah at Kid World, she wondered what a mother would feel, letting go of her child like this for the first time. During the day, she thought about Tobrah's parting glance. She seemed calm, not afraid or shy, as if she were used to being dumped somewhere strange. At the end of the day, Mrs. Fields, the day-care director, told Jackie that Tobrah had a high energy level and tended to be bossy. "Her cooperative-play attributes need attention," the woman said. At a table alone, Tobrah was engrossed in coloring a Xeroxed pig red. Her jeans and T-shirt were dirty and her hair was tangled.

When they arrived at the house, Tobrah ran straight to her room. Jackie could hear her from the kitchen, where she was unloading the groceries. Tobrah was talking to her toys. "I told you to stay right there! But you've been up dancing. I said you couldn't dance. But all you want to do is dance!"

In the doorway, Jackie watched Tobrah dash the doll and the bear around, banging them together until the doll's hat fell off. After she had whipped their behinds and threatened them with no supper, she placed them back on the pillow and gave them new orders.

"No dancing. No walking around!"

Jackie had been married twice, once in her twenties and once in her thirties. The husbands were a blur. The first, Carl, was generous but immature. He saw Jackie and himself as a "fun couple." Her second husband, Jerry, was quiet and sweet, but he hid too much—an attachment to his mother, his secret drawer, even lapses of memory. He frightened her when he began locking himself in the bathroom for hours. She still saw him around town, and they spoke cordially, much the way they had done when they lived together. For the past several years now, she had been going with Bob Burns. They had an understanding. They knew their relationship was wrong according to the church they attended together, but they decided that the legality of marriage was really just a piece of paper. They had worked that out in their minds, and it left them free to love each other, Jackie thought. She wanted to keep up with the times, within reason.

"I can't spend the weekend at your apartment," she told Bob on the telephone a couple of weeks after Tobrah's arrival. "You'll have to come here. I can't drag her around everywhere. I want her to know where she lives."

"Are you sure you want me there? I might just confuse her."

"No. Come on over. I need you."

Bob still wore the same size jeans he wore in high school and even had an old pair to prove it. He golfed and didn't drink. He was divorced and had two grown daughters, one in the Air Force and the other in Louisville, pregnant. He seemed to find becoming a grandfather a spooky idea, and Jackie had been nervous about how he would adjust to her new situation. As they spoke on the phone now, she gazed at the decal of a brightly colored unicorn she had put low on a window for Tobrah. Nowadays, Jackie seemed to dwell on things she hadn't noticed before—small things at a child's eye level, like the napkin holder and the cabinet-door handles. She tried to tell Bob about this. She said, "It makes me think about Jack Frost. Remember those beautiful designs in the windows? Is that something only kids see? I used to see them at my grandmother's."

"Jack Frost doesn't come around anymore."

"How come? Pollution?"

"No. Double-glazed windows and central heating. You saw Jack Frost in old, uninsulated houses where the windows were a single layer of glass. The frost was moisture condensed on the inside."

"I'm amazed. Is that supposed to be progress?"

She always counted on Bob to know things.

When he came over that Friday, he was anxious, fuming over something that had happened on the job. He said, "I waited at the loading platform for an hour and a half for this bozo to show up and then come to find out he's with his girlfriend at the mall picking out a china pattern. He forgot to bring the shipment over."

"I imagine he had more important things on his mind than a load of cement," said Jackie, taking his cap from his hand. He always took it off indoors, a fact she found interesting and unusual. Most men she knew wore their caps with almost fanatic devotion, indoors and out.

"You can't count on young people these days," said Bob as he searched for a Band-Aid in Jackie's medicine cabinet. He had a paper-cut from junk mail.

"Young people? Why, you're not so old! I hope when I'm fifty I don't feel like my life is over."

After supper, while Jackie was washing the dishes, Tobrah suddenly started flattening pillows on the couch with a spatula.

"Beat 'em good, hon," said Jackie. "They need it."

"I'm going out to the drugstore to get some antihistamines," Bob said, looking for his cap. "Does anybody want to come?"

"Are you allergic to something here?" asked Jackie.

"No. My nose has been itching all day."

"If your nose itches it means somebody's coming with a hole in his britches," Jackie said teasingly.

"I've got a hole in my britches," said Tobrah, giggling.

Bob pulled on his cap. "Are y'all coming?"

Jackie said, "No, we've got work to do." She found a second spatula in the kitchen and started whacking the drapes. "The hard part is the places up high," she said to Tobrah.

"Aren't you supposed to beat rugs outside?" Bob asked as he went out the door. They were hitting the couch, the chairs, the shag rug. On their hands and knees, they smacked the rug, sending up fibers and dust.

Jackie sneezed and Tobrah said, "This is fun." Jackie experienced a rushing sensation of blissful abandon, something she'd thought only a child could feel. She remembered feeling this way once when she was small—the meaningless happiness of jumping up and down on a bed, bouncing off the walls, chanting, "Little Bo Peep is fast asleep."

Tobrah had a way of moving jerkily—as if she were imitating some old comedian or mocking a private memory. She skipped ahead down the strawberry rows, then stopped to pluck a bright berry.

"Gotcha!" she cried. She had picked up the expression at Kid World and had been applying it to everything.

Jackie's friend Annabelle had brought them to a farm south of town to pick strawberries. It was the last of the crop and the patch was drying out. Tobrah had been collecting all sorts of berries—green ones, deformed ones, rotten ones, as well as ripe ones. Jackie felt warm and peaceful. Tobrah's tan skin glowed bright in the hot morning sun, and now and then she tugged at a handful of hair, stretching the curls.

"Don't pick the green ones," Jackie said, but Tobrah didn't hear. Jackie said to Annabelle, "I'm not sure when to correct her or when to just let her go."

"Wait till she starts school," Annabelle said sympathetically. "You won't be able to keep up with her."

"She's always busy with something," said Jackie. "She's got a great attention span."

"She must not have seen much TV."

"I don't know. She won't tell much."

"She's repressing her grief." Annabelle worked in the typing pool at a social services agency and liked to talk knowledgeably about the cases she had typed up.

"What does a little child know about grief?" Jackie asked. She threw a rotten berry across a couple of rows.

Annabelle shook her head skeptically. "You can take a child that's been through a trauma and give it all the love in the world and it might take years for the child to start to trust you."

"That's ridiculous."

Instantly, Jackie regretted her tone. Annabelle's son was in a chemical-dependency program, and Jackie knew Annabelle blamed herself. But Jackie felt as though some kind of safety valve had broken in her. She was becoming impatient with adult ideas. All she wanted to do was play with Tobrah. They had been reading—stacks and stacks of storybooks from the library. Tobrah was rapidly learning to recognize words. They watched videotapes together. They made paper villages and building-block malls, with paper dolls as shoppers. They were collecting stuffed animals, yard-sale bargains. Yesterday they had a tea party. Tobrah had wrapped a ball of yarn around the table and chairs, making a large green spiderweb. Jackie had to cut it apart, and the yarn—five dollars' worth—was ruined. When Jackie was a child, she would have been punished for wasting yarn, but now she couldn't even scold Tobrah. Jackie was too much amazed that anyone would have thought of draping yarn in that fashion. It was a creation.

Now Tobrah was coming toward her, where Jackie was working her hands through strawberry plants. A spider jumped off a leaf. Jackie looked up. Tobrah, clutching several red berries, had red stains on her mouth. Her hair was bright in the loud sun.

"I want to go," she whined. "I'm hot."

"I'm ready," Annabelle said. "My handy's full."

After they took their handies of strawberries to the owner's house to pay, they poured the berries into large metal pots and plastic dishpans they had brought. Carefully, Jackie set the pans of berries in the back seat of the car, next to Tobrah. Jackie fastened the seat belt for her. As she clasped the buckle and pulled the belt tight, Tobrah's fingernail accidentally scratched against Jackie's wrist, drawing blood. It had never occurred to Jackie that a child's fingernails would need to be trimmed. She stared at the little nails, transparent as fish scales.

"Does she remind you of when I was little?" Jackie asked her mother.

"You weren't that sure of yourself."

"Do you think I looked like her?"

"I can't see you in her. Maybe I don't want to. All I see is him."

Lorraine paused from glazing a cake to light a cigarette. She tapped it on the counter the way Jackie remembered her father doing his unfiltered Luckies. Lucky Strikes. LSMFT, she recalled, from out of nowhere. Lorraine, in a voice hoarse from smoking, said, "Believe me, she's better off without her daddy."

"Why are you still so bitter?"

"I reckon I want to be. It's my privilege."

Jackie ducked her mother's smoke stream. "Did you hate Daddy?"

"I guess I did, finally. I made him go. I couldn't stand it anymore. He was always complaining, never enjoying anything." Lorraine shuddered. "That was the worst part. He was such a sourpuss. He thought he was better than anybody else. He was always growling about the way the world was going to hell. You can't put up with people like that."

Jackie stood over Tobrah, searching for resemblances between herself and the sleeping child. She could see a faint repetition of her own upper lip, the narrow forehead, a certain dark shadow under her eyes. Jackie had heard that computers could create new faces by combining photographs. It amused her to imagine Meg Ryan crossed with Sylvester Stallone; Newt Gingrich and Monica Lewinsky. Sensations from her own childhood floated forth; the taste of grapes from the trellis in the backyard, the sour green tang of the pulp set off by the sweet purple lining of the skin; the sandy texture of a pink marshmallow bunny squatting in Easter grass; the distasteful odor of sloppy joes in the first-grade lunchroom.

Bob was supposed to visit, but he was late and Tobrah had fallen asleep. He had taken his mother to town. It was Social-

Security-check day. His mother didn't drive, and since his father's death, Bob ran errands for her and took her places. His mother kept asking them what his arrangement with Jackie was called. She said she couldn't keep track of the new alternatives to marriage. When Bob and Jackie and Tobrah showed up at church together one Sunday, Bob's mother was embarrassed, and the congregation itself seemed shaken. Jackie hadn't been back to church with Tobrah since then.

Bob came in at ten minutes after nine, bringing ice cream for Tobrah—pistachio, because of the color.

"She's already asleep," said Jackie. "She ate a hot dog, but I haven't eaten yet. I waited for you—the pot roast is drying out though."

"I like it dried out," he said with a grin. "Like jerky."

"Oh, you're just saying that."

"No, it's true!"

"You know what Tobrah said? She said bananas smell like fingernail polish." Jackie thrust a banana under his nose and he sniffed it. "Isn't that funny?"

"She's right," Bob said, sniffing the banana again.

He set the ice cream in the freezer and swiped his finger through the whipped cream in a bowl on the counter. Jackie was making a sinful dessert.

"I think childhood has changed," Jackie said. "The way I remember it, any kid who said that about bananas would just be laughed at, but nowadays they call it 'creative.' "

"True," Bob said. "What I remember is how everything you thought about depended on what you could afford. Nowadays kids have everything, so their minds just run wild."

"Yeah. The sky's the limit." Jackie slapped down place mats. "I don't understand it," she said. "I don't understand where it all leads."

After supper, they watched TV in her bedroom. Jackie was

afraid Tobrah would catch them in bed. Tonight they watched a videotape of *The Big Easy* that Jackie had rented that afternoon. The movie had a remarkably sexy scene, but neither of them stirred. It was after midnight when the movie ended, and they still had their clothes on.

"I'll be back in a minute," said Jackie, starting to get out of bed. "I'm going to check on Tobrah."

Bob caught her arm. "You check on babies—not five-year-old girls."

"I want to see if that fan is too much air for her." She flinched. "Do you think I'm being too protective?"

"I'm afraid you'll let yourself get too attached to her." He reached his arm around her tenderly. "Kids are a mess," he said. "They always know how to hurt you." He shooed a curl away from her forehead.

"But Dad gave her to me. Maybe that was his way of making up to me after all these years." She sat up straight against the backrest. "The bastard," she said. "He left me when I wasn't much older than Tobrah. And now he ups and leaves her too. Well, we'll show *him*!"

"You're going a little overboard, Jackie."

"Bull noodles! What has my life amounted to? No kids. Two lousy marriages. I'm sure it was his fault, ruining things right at the start."

"You're too hard on yourself, Jackie," Bob said. "Maybe you shouldn't be the one to bring her up."

She opened her paperback. Words raced before her eyes. She was barely conscious of the book, wondering if it was upside down. She saw herself sitting there, not concentrating, not grasping what was in the book or what was going on with Bob. Tobrah and Bob and Jackie, an oddball little family. Jackie pictured them in a movie—the wacky mom, the long-suffering dad, the precocious child. Or, the desperate mom, the sad-sack dad, the devil child.

✦ ✦ ✦

Jackie usually slept late on weekends, and one Saturday she woke up to find that Tobrah had eaten most of a jar of peanut butter. Jackie didn't know what prevented the child from walking out the door, running away. Sometimes the little girl seemed filled with secret knowledge—probably only stuff learned from TV, Jackie thought—and at other times she seemed to have just come out of a hole. Her favorite books were *The Hungry Princess* and *The Foolish Cat*, which Jackie thought were for younger children, but she wasn't sure anymore what was appropriate. At the grocery one day, Tobrah had wanted to buy cat food and stationery, and Jackie had had to stop and try to think why they couldn't buy them. Jackie started liking pizzas and tacos, kid food. One evening they even had fluffer-nutters and Cokes for supper. That was Tobrah's worst day at Kid World. Melissa McKay had come with her My Little Pony and wouldn't let anybody comb its tail. Several of the children had broken into tears.

After supper, Tobrah soberly colored in her coloring book, working with fierce concentration. The crayons lay scattered on the kitchen table. As Tobrah shifted position, a dandelion crayon rolled over the edge of the table. Jackie caught it. Tobrah was coloring a ballerina surrounded by clowns. She explained, "This lady is telling the clowns about her comb she lost, and they said the man that found the comb would be a prince. If she could find him and he had the comb she would be a princess."

"That sounds like Cinderella."

Tobrah shook her head vigorously. "This lady don't have any mean sisters. Nobody makes her work."

"But Cinderella wanted to work," said Jackie. "Cinderella decided not to marry the prince. She decided to go to medical school and be a doctor."

"No, she didn't! You always tell it that way. You don't tell it right."

"Everybody has to work," Jackie said, rolling a sepia crayon between her fingers. "My mother worked at the same plant where I work. She had to be on her feet eight hours a day. And she didn't have a prince. It was just her and me."

"Can we have a gerbil?"

They had seen gerbils in a pet store the day before.

"We can't have pets here. It's not allowed in a house this small."

Jackie felt guilty about the lie, but she couldn't imagine cleaning up after an animal. She remembered the summer days when her mother went off to work and left her alone. She was really too young to be left alone. She watched TV and listened to records and played solitaire. She hadn't minded. She liked it. Nobody bothered her. Tobrah never seemed lonely either. It pleased Jackie to recognize this kinship with her sister. She remembered playing by herself, working on long, absorbing projects. Her paper dolls lived in shoe-box houses on a cardboard street, with house plants for trees. She had created a whole town once, with streets made of neckties and stores full of tiny objects (thimbles, buttons, and candy). The names came drifting back to her. Mulberry Street, Primrose Street. The town was named Wellsville, because nobody ever got sick there. Jackie had had pneumonia the winter before she built Wellsville.

"Jackie, jack-in-the-box, Jackie O," said Tobrah now.

"How do you know jack-in-the-box?" asked Jackie. "And what do you mean by Jackie O?"

"Jackie Jackie Jackie," Tobrah chanted, shifting her attention to some cassette tapes Jackie had been organizing in a shoe box. Tobrah's green sweatshirt featured new snags and smears of chocolate syrup.

✦   ✦   ✦

A month later, Jackie realized she might be pregnant. The notion seemed absurd—it was too ridiculously coincidental for a five-year-old to enter her life, followed so soon by a baby. But Jackie was thrilled, eager to believe it. She felt stirred up. Silent with her secret, she shopped with friends and in the mornings went walking with women in the subdivision, for exercise. She woke up early, waiting for that stir of nausea that was supposed to come, but she felt only anticipation. She felt as if her blood had been carbonated.

By the time of her doctor's appointment, Jackie calculated that she could be six weeks pregnant. She took an early-morning urine specimen with her—in a jelly jar, enclosed politely in a paper sack. She had read in a women's magazine that she should do this. The same magazine said that having a baby late in life was a healthy way of rejuvenating the system.

"I appreciate that," the doctor said briskly as he set the sack aside. "But we don't do those anymore. We do blood tests instead. They're more accurate."

It bothered Jackie that scientific knowledge seemed to change like fashion trends.

As a nurse explored her arm, trying to find a vein, the doctor said, "It would be highly unusual at your age, especially if you've never been pregnant before. Still, healthy babies have been born to women your age." By his tone, Jackie thought he may as well have said, "People your age have been said to sprout wings and fly. But I've personally never seen it."

The tube attached to the needle was enormous. Her blood was dark, almost black. As she felt the blood rush into the tube, a wave of nausea hit her and she saw the room go dim. She tried to think of something peaceful. Her stomach knotted.

"We'll dispose of that urine sample for you," the nurse said.

After work, Jackie picked up Tobrah at day care. Tobrah had been getting premium stars almost every day. "She's just original, not screwed up," Jackie had informed Annabelle. Tobrah was sitting at a table, her head bent over a finger painting. Splotches of blue paint streaked her face. Swabbing at the paint on Tobrah's cheek, Jackie said, "Hey, that's not your color. Your color is green."

On the way home they stopped at the videotape store. Jackie held Tobrah's hand as they crossed the shopping-center parking lot. At the curb Tobrah burst free, and then inside the store she stared at a woman on crutches.

"Don't stare," Jackie said quietly.

Tobrah whispered, "I think she fell out of an airplane."

"Where did you get such an idea?"

Tobrah was already looking at videotape boxes on display.

"Let's see *The Love Bug*," Jackie suggested.

Tobrah made a "yuck" face. "I want to see *E.T.*"

"But we've seen that twice. Don't you want to see something else?"

To avoid a scene, Jackie abruptly checked out *E.T.* She didn't want anything to spoil the evening. She felt almost romantic about it. Once or twice she felt fleeting, squirming sensations inside her abdomen. She didn't want Bob to know. It was too private.

During the movie, Jackie kept her eyes on Tobrah's activities—coloring pictures, dressing her doll, beating her heels against the couch, searching under the couch cushions for lost doll jewelry. The little girl seemed self-possessed, as if each small action had a meaning and intention. Jackie knew Tobrah was haphazardly testing out the world, but she wondered if the little girl was actually being brave, in the face of the knowledge that she was an orphan. As Tobrah recited dialogue along with the movie, Jackie washed the popcorn bowls and put away the popper. She found a half-popped kernel in her shirt pocket.

At the end of the movie, Jackie grabbed Tobrah, squeezing her in an urgent hug.

"Who do you love?" she asked, but Tobrah squirmed, pushing her away.

A Tinkertoy wheel skittered across the kitchen floor, making tap-shoe sounds.

The next afternoon, during her break, Jackie called the clinic for the results of the test.

The doctor said, "You're not pregnant." He paused, then said, "We could run some hormonal studies to see what's going on. My guess is that you're going through normal midlife changes."

Jackie saw a supervisor pass by with a cup of coffee. The coffee sloshed on the floor but he didn't notice. The man didn't even realize he had spilled it on his pants.

She slammed the receiver so hard it jumped off the hook. The sudden dial tone was like a siren.

Jackie and Tobrah walked the full length of the mall, stopping at every store that interested Tobrah. The little girl was enthralled, but Jackie, in a daze, hardly noticed what was before her. Tobrah ate pizza, drank an Orange Julius, got a bag of Gummi Bears. They tried on sneakers, looked unsuccessfully for a My Little Pony purse, cruised through a store of kitchen paraphernalia, caressed piles of summer cotton sweaters and T-shirts, hit every toy section.

"I had a good time," Tobrah said in the car on the way home. She might have been a little visitor, politely thanking her hostess.

"Where did you learn to say that?" Jackie couldn't imagine her father as a model of good manners.

Tobrah didn't answer. She played with a cassette tape, opening and closing the plastic box. She opened the glove compartment and shut it. It was growing dark, and the Friday-night traffic swirled around them. Ahead, a car made a sudden left turn in front of an oncoming SUV. The night was alive, full of lights and speed, and Tobrah was straining against her shoulder harness, moving in the seat restlessly, as if she had to see everything.

At the house, the telephone was ringing as they came through the door. It was Bob, wanting to know what they were doing. He was excited. "Let's all go to the Bigfoot competition over in Sikeston tomorrow. We can take the camper and spend the night."

"I can't think about it right now. We were at the mall and we're tired."

"I'll bring a cooler and we'll get some barbecue."

"I'm afraid if we take Tobrah, you'll get stressed out."

"Don't be silly! Me and Tobrah are buddies."

"Those monster trucks might scare her."

"Kids love that stuff. Hey, Jackie, you're making excuses. You need to get ahold of yourself."

"Everybody seems to know what I need."

"Let's do it. We'll start out early and make a day of it. I'll pick you up at eight o'clock."

"I don't really want to go."

"Did I do something wrong?"

"No. I can't explain. I'm just tired." Jackie realized that if she had been pregnant, she definitely wouldn't have told Bob—not for a while anyway. Did all women feel this, that they had to shut everyone else out when it came to their love for a child?

With Bob still insisting he was coming over early, Jackie said good-bye, then noticed the mail she had brought in. There was a letter from someone named Carnahan in Arkansas. She didn't know anyone in Arkansas.

Dear Miss Holmes,
My sister was Becky Songs Holmes, Toborah's mother. My sister was deceased on August 8 of last year (cancer). I understand you have custody due to terms in Ed Holmeses' will. In the interest of the child, I am applying to be her legal guardian. I can give Toborah the home she deserves. My husband and I have three children—ages eight, ten, and twelve, and Toborah would be the youngest. I'm sure they would be happy to have a new little sister. We have met Toborah before, when my dear sister passed away, and we did not want to take the little child from her daddy. He seemed to need her so much after losing his wife. We have only just now heard about her daddy's unfortunate fat and heard how Toborah was taken to Kentucky.

Fat? A typo, Jackie realized. But Toborah? She continued reading details of the arrangements to have "Toborah" brought to Arkansas, and what they had to offer: her own room, a dog, a brother and sisters. Mr. Carnahan was a textile worker, and his wife, Linda, who wrote the letter, worked for the telephone company. The letter was so pretty. Jackie was overwhelmed by its authority. But the one little mistake blew it. Jackie wadded the letter and tossed it into the wastebasket. She ran water into a plastic jug and watered the plants. She cleaned up the sink and loaded the dishwasher. With a paper towel she wiped up a spot of cranberry-juice drink from the floor. Then she heard Tobrah in the bathtub, splashing and singing loudly, playing.

"Stand up," Tobrah was saying. "Your hands against the wall."

Jackie hurried down the hall to check on her. She didn't know at what age a child could take a bath alone. She had been so unprepared. Tobrah was like a dream, a desire for a child—a desperate wish that had come to Jackie late in life. She had to catch up somehow, read some textbooks, do it right.

Jackie was up before sunrise, packing a small bag. She hurried Tobrah out of bed, through a bowl of cereal, then into the car. She drove toward the lake, forty miles east. After the sky grew light, they stopped at a mini-mart. Jackie had coffee and a muffin, and Tobrah had a doughnut. By eight o'clock, when Bob would be pulling up at her house, they had reached the lake. It was a place Jackie had visited many times, years ago, between husbands. It used to seem peaceful and vacant, without variety or possibility. It had soothed her because it made no demands on her. But now it seemed charged with life, confusing and complicated. A coal-filled barge headed toward the locks. A flock of birds flew over noisily, like a cheering section. Pleasure boats were already shooting through the water.

At the nature center they got a brochure with maps of the trails. Jackie guided Tobrah down a short trail called the Waterfowl Loop. They saw geese gathered at the shore. As they approached, the geese trundled into the water like pull toys.

Tobrah said, "A mother goose takes off flying backwards to teach its baby goose not to fall. If you fly backwards, you can't never fall."

She flapped her arms and ran backwards.

"Watch where you're going, honey," said Jackie, reaching out to catch her.

Three deer enclosed in a pen moved shyly away from the fence, as Tobrah staggered past and whirled to a stop. She stared at the deer. Later, outside the nature center, Jackie and Tobrah saw a small owl tethered to a post. The owl swiveled his neck, his eyes following them curiously, like anxious moons. Jackie imagined that he was amazed by the sight of Tobrah. The park ranger stared at her, too. People would think the child was hers, Jackie thought. They might think that she had been with some strange man and created this child. She wished it were true.

The ranger said, "At night we take the owl inside so a great horned owl won't swoop down and get him."

"What's his name?" Jackie said.

"We don't give the wildlife names here because we don't want to encourage keeping wild animals as pets."

Inside the nature center they saw stuffed animals. A ranger stationed there said, "All the animals you see here were road-kills. That bobcat was a road-kill from last summer. He weighed twenty-two pounds, I'd say."

"I want a kitty like that," said Tobrah.

"My mother's cat is part wildcat," a fat woman said to the ranger. "He's got those whiskers and big cheeks." She puffed out her own cheeks, becoming the cat for an instant.

"I don't believe a bobcat would ever mate with a house cat," said the ranger.

"Well, you might change your mind if you saw my mother's cat," said the woman indignantly.

Jackie smiled and squeezed Tobrah's hand. Tobrah jerked away. Her body was tensed, trembling—almost, Jackie thought, as though she were on the verge of a convulsion.

"What is it, Tobrah?" Jackie asked anxiously, squatting down to look into the child's face.

"Kitty," Tobrah said, in a voice as close to despair as Jackie had ever heard. Tears rolled down Tobrah's cheeks.

Jackie held her close and tried to soothe her. In a few minutes Tobrah was over the outburst, and by the time they reached the car, she seemed to have forgotten about the cat. It was just something Tobrah thought she wanted, but she could live without it, Jackie told herself. A child's whim. Who wasn't a child? she wondered. Adulthood was a role people played. They forgot that they were just pretending. It was all bluff and fluff. A man at work used to say his long-haired orange tomcat was all "bluff and fluff." He would say it a couple of times a week, as if trying to convince everyone of his superiority over his cat, a pathetic thing for someone to have to do.

She had parked the car in the shade, and some gummy pollen had dotted the windshield. She wiped at it with a tissue. Tobrah was singing to herself, echoing the birdsong from the woods. A pickup angled into a nearby parking spot.

When her father wrecked his pickup, he was probably driving recklessly, childishly, Jackie thought. He took her to the carnival once, she remembered, and she rode the bumper cars. He thrust a cloud of cotton candy into her hand and left her at the bumper cars with a string of tickets while he flirted with a woman at the merry-go-round ticket booth. For an hour, Jackie rode, bumping and steering with devilish glee, happy with her freedom. Her father disappeared from sight. Her steering wheel was sticky from the cotton candy. When he came back for her, all he said was, "I'll bet you qualify for a driver's license by now, Little Bean." She had forgotten that nickname until now, and she didn't know where it came from.

Tobrah got in the car, crushing a paper cup in the seat. Without being told, she fastened her seat belt, fumbling for only a moment.

"I'm ready," she said.

Tunica

Liz had the sebaceous cysts removed from her head the day before her trip to the casinos down in Tunica. The five bumps were small, requiring only a stitch each, so afterward she wasn't sure they were relevant to her fortune. The dermatologist's name, ironically, was Harry. She couldn't keep a straight face while he performed the operation, which was almost pleasant. There was something erotic about the feathery sensations of having her numbed scalp slit and tugged. It felt like a cat licking her hand.

With the deadened spots on her head tickling into life, she drove across town to her mother's house, the radio blaring a group called Pit Bulls on Crack. She felt ebullient, like a lightbulb about to pop. She honked at a Buick spraddled across an intersection, then hit the horn an extra giddy blast. Whenever she felt the smoldering fire inside her about to burst into flame, she knew it was time to head for Tunica.

Her friends frequently instructed her on what she ought to do—like file a restraining order against her husband, sign up for kick boxing, join some support group or other—but Liz stubbornly resisted. Everybody had an answer and a twelve-step program. There were more answers than questions anymore, she believed.

She swung into her parents' neighborhood, a claustrophobic little cluster of FHA-financed houses. Her mother's rust-bucket Cutlass blocked the carport, so Liz had to park on the street. Through the glass of the kitchen storm door, she saw her mother, Julie, on the telephone. When Liz entered, Julie said to the telephone, "I've got to go. My daughter's just come in from having her head worked on—these knots that run in families? It's the knottiest bunch of people I ever saw. I always say I married a knothead."

"Who was that?" asked Liz as her mother cradled the receiver.

"Oh, somebody from a phone outfit trying to sell me their package deal."

"You were on a *junk* call?"

"They said I could get long distance cheaper than what I'm getting."

"Who do you ever call long distance?"

"Well, maybe I *would* call somebody if it was cheaper," Julie said. She grabbed a sponge and came at Liz, as if she intended to wipe her off. "I've got some bad news," she said. "Peyton's mama's in the hospital. She had a stroke and is in a coma."

Liz's mind zigzagged as she listened to Julie fill in the medical details about Daisy, Liz's mother-in-law. Daisy was not so old, but she smoked heavily and lived on deep-fried cuisine. Liz grabbed the sponge from her mother and set it on the toaster.

"How bad is it?" she asked.

"Bad. Peyton said if you were there, maybe she'd come to."

The idea threw her. "Does he think I'm some kind of faith healer? He never had any faith in me."

"Don't get smart. Peyton needs you with him at a time like this."

"Well, I don't need him," Liz said. "I've written him out of my script."

If her mother knew the truth about Peyton, she would not have made such a suggestion, Liz thought. She wished she had driven straight to Tunica and learned about Daisy later. She dreaded seeing Peyton, and she had always been uncomfortable around her mother-in-law, who judged her by her clothing. Before saying hello, Daisy always eyed her up and down.

Julie said, "Here, let me see that head." She poked through Liz's short hair. "Why, they didn't shave a hair."

"They don't do that anymore," said Liz, wriggling away. "And they don't let you keep the knots. They send them off to the lab so they can charge you more."

"You used to could make a bracelet out of your gallstones," Julie said. "I was looking forward to that if I ever got gallstones."

"You can cancel that little dream," Liz said. "It's probably against the law now."

Liz and Peyton had separated six months ago, when he went to jail for possession of cocaine. By the time he was released (prematurely, in her opinion), she had decided she could be free of him. She wouldn't allow him to stay in the house, so he moved into a small apartment above a friend's auto-body shop and got work laying sewer pipes. Liz had made Peyton take all his tools and tackle and videotapes. His gun collection had already been confiscated when he was arrested—the shotgun in the closet, the Weatherby .243 varmint rifle over the mantel, and the handguns in various drawers. Now she wouldn't even call him when she needed his vise grip to open a stuck window lock. For jar lids she used a "rubber husband," a gimmick that came free with a set of stemware. But Peyton was a nagging presence, like the shotgun that had been propped in the closet. He had begun to leave threatening messages on her answering machine. He swore revenge and demanded that she behave like a wife. "You belong to me," he had said.

At home Liz ignored the new messages on her answering machine and opened a beer to settle her head. She microwaved some popcorn and watched a romantic made-for-TV movie, trying to pretend she didn't know about Daisy's stroke. She badly wanted to go to Tunica on the excursion bus at dawn. Gambling was her way of mocking the dull predictability of her life, and Daisy's stroke—an actual surprise—confused her.

When the telephone rang, she didn't answer. Her caller I.D. showed Peyton's number, and when she heard his wheedling voice on the answering machine, she lowered the volume. She wanted to keep Peyton away until after Tunica. He would need petting and forgiveness, and she didn't feel capable of offering any. Although she had thrown out his *Guns & Ammo* magazines, there were still reminders of him in the house. Stuffing extruded from holes in the couch, worn from five years of TV evenings with Peyton. She had once hoped they could have a nicer place someday, and she had imagined decorating it with country-kitchen antique-style milk jugs and egg baskets and calico-print chickens. When she married him, she felt exhilarated at each new purchase. But their furniture was cheap, and it wore down at about the same rate as their marriage, faster than the payment schedules. Now she thought about the way he used to sit in front of the TV, a gun in his lap. He would be taking it apart, putting it back together, as if it needed exercise to remain operable. She remembered him caressing the barrel, loving on it as one would fondle a baby. Night after night, Peyton sat watching TV with one of his guns astride his lap—dismantling and reassembling it, concentrating hard.

Peyton had roared into her life. She was seventeen and he was twenty-four. He seemed mysterious, as if his pockets were loaded with taboos, like candy treats. She fell for him because he was a stud—wearing studs and black leather and frenzied hair and a pair of motorcycle boots that could stomp her heart into submission. He was comfortable in his body, with a cock of the head that implied a secret, superior knowledge—his crotch still warm from the heat of his Harley. The way he moved—casual, unhurried, luxuriating in his muscularity—called to her, like an evangelist inviting her to come forward and get her soul saved. She didn't know he was a drug dealer. He quit for her sake, he told her later, but she soon decided she had married too young, a mistake that delineated her life as clearly as an arranged marriage in a remote culture. When she began working nights, she felt relieved that she wouldn't have to watch the revenge thrillers he had begun renting. Then he drifted into trouble, back into dealing. It was so easy, he told her, he couldn't stay away from it. It beckoned him, like a lighthouse. "You never saw a lighthouse in your life," Liz pointed out.

Now the telephone rang again. She picked popcorn hulls out of her teeth. In a commercial, a farmer was walking with his dog in a field of soybeans. The fields were green and pretty, edged with mist. The video whizzed through scenes of the man's life—his marriage, the birth of a baby, then his daughter's wedding, with her wedding dress whirling among the bushy plants. The commercial was for a weed killer for no-till soybeans. It made farm life look rich and grand and satisfying. But it also made a life span seem as short as a season's crop.

In the morning, as she stepped out of the shower, she heard the telephone ringing and almost burst into tears, thinking of Peyton's mother, who always looked fresh as a daisy—however fresh that was. Daisies actually smelled like vomit. The telephone stopped ringing.

At the shopping center, the bus was packed with senior citizens and several lone eccentrics Liz recognized from earlier trips. She found a seat near the rear of the bus and shoved her tote bag on the floor against the wall. She was dressed in her new wide-legged shorts, with a tight tank-top and a loose poppy-print shirt. In her bag was a fleece throw, in case she got cold on the bus.

Suddenly Peyton slid into the seat beside her, startling her. He had tracked her down with his bad news. Waves of goose bumps rippled across her skin.

"Where were you?" he asked. "I was at the hospital all night."

"Is she all right?"

"She's still in a coma."

She sat quietly as he told her about the nightmarish night at the hospital and the doctors' cryptic, noncommittal comments. His hard shoulder pressed against her. His plaid shirt was fresh, but his jeans had twin rips above the knees. He was wearing the jeans with the Confederate flag patch on the right thigh.

"What do you think you're doing, Liz?" he asked. "Your mama said you needed to be with me. She told me you were going to Tunica to blow your paycheck." He slapped her bare knee.

"Don't touch me," she said.

"I'm coming with you."

"You would leave your sick mother to go play the slots?"

"You need me to go along with you—for your own good."

"I don't need you to chaperone. I *told* you I wrote you out of my script."

"Hey, I like them shorts of yours." He poked her thigh, making a motion like a mole snouting through dirt. She knocked his hand away with her fist.

She didn't know what to say. Peyton had always neglected his mother, so Liz wasn't surprised that he would duck out now. As the bus lurched out of the parking lot, Peyton tilted his seat back and adjusted the bill of his cap to shade his brow. He reminded Liz of a character in a movie, one of those criminals played by a handsome actor with a smirk. His cobra-head tattoo peeked out of his shirt sleeve. She hadn't missed that at all.

"How come you're off work?" he asked.

"I'm working twelve-hour shifts now, so I get more days off."

"They cut your hours," he said.

"But I got a raise—a dollar an hour." Liz watched for the sun, which was on the verge of rising behind Wal-Mart. "You're ruining my day," she said. "You ought to go stay with your mom." She had no idea what he was feeling about Daisy.

"I'll be good," Peyton said, patting her leg. "I won't get in your way."

"I'm not loaning you any money when you lose yours. As far as I'm concerned, you're on your own."

"I won't go near the blackjack tables," he said. "Where were you yesterday? I tried to call. I went by the house."

Liz shrugged. "Had my knots cut out—don't touch my head."

"Won't your brains ooze out?" He flashed one of his Three Stooges smirks.

Peyton was bleary-eyed and fuzzy-faced. In jail he had lost weight. Actually, he looked good, Liz thought, since he grew his hair back. In jail, he experimented with shaving his head, but it looked peculiar.

"Did you see that guy in the second row?" Peyton asked rather loudly. "His blubber hangs off into the aisle. I can see it all the way back here. People like that should just be put out of their misery."

"Don't be stupid."

"Well, I say it's time to rid the world of blubber-butts. And queers. And liberals. And people who drive Lincoln Navigators. And David Letterman."

"That kind of talk gets old," she said angrily. "Decent people don't talk that way anymore."

"Chill out, babe. You've been watching too much television." He gave her knee a little squeeze.

She had never figured out how to talk to him when he got like this. "At least I haven't been in jail," she said finally.

"One of these days you'll come to a bad end, Liz."

"Speak for yourself." She opened her magazine.

"Mama wanted us to stay together," he whispered in her ear. "She just couldn't bear knowing how we turned out. I believe that's why she had a stroke."

"That wouldn't cause a stroke."

"I think you still love me," Peyton said. "I'm coming home with you tonight," he said. "To *our* bed. I miss you. Can't you see I'm full of hurt? And now my mama's dying. Are you going to kick me when I'm down?"

She wouldn't answer. She flipped magazine pages.

"You're not getting away with this any longer," he said.

They sat in silence for a while, Liz fuming. Peyton was in-

terfering with her new mission to straighten out her life—
which she could not have explained to him even if she had a
week's time. Now apparently they were running away together, and everyone would blame them for abandoning
Daisy on her deathbed.

As the bus approached the confluence of the Ohio River
and the Mississippi, Liz could see the famous ninety-five-
foot steel cross towering in the distance. It appeared to ex-
tend a frightening embrace in all directions. After crossing
the rivers, the bus headed south toward Arkansas. Peyton,
slouching beside her, seemed to be sleeping. To steady her
mind, Liz worked a word-search puzzle in the magazine she
had brought. While he was in jail, she had felt tranquil, but
she couldn't focus on what her future held; it seemed like a
fragile bubble that popped when she tried to visualize it. She
hadn't expected him to become so possessive after she threw
him out. He made her feel that she was unjustly finding fault.
One day a couple of years before, some cops were beating a
suspect on the TV news, and Peyton said, "Goddamn, why
didn't they just kick his head in while they were at it?" It
shocked her into reassessing his brutal swagger. She had
thought it was typical male bluster; he was cool, spouting his
charges at the world. But that day she saw him differently.
He seemed small and pathetic. It takes a while to know a person, she kept telling herself.

Peyton slept beside her, not waking until they crossed the
Mississippi River again, at Memphis. When he stirred, she
turned to peer out the window at plow-scarred fields. After
Memphis, the delta stretched out flat and blank—old cotton
fields waiting to be submerged under something new and
transforming. Billboards planted in the fields like scarecrows
marked the way to the casinos. In the distance the casinos
began to appear, rising out of the fields like ocean vessels on
the horizon—a Confederate armada positioned along the

Mississippi, protecting the delta from northern invaders. In this misty atmosphere, Liz thought, the casinos seemed to really float. By law, they were supposed to operate offshore, but their floating was illusory. They actually stood on solid ground a mile or more from the river. She didn't understand a law like that. It sounded slippery, a lie that let the casinos cut loose and glide along an imaginary river. She didn't trust the law. It hadn't been enough to work the kinks out of Peyton. Now she was afraid she couldn't get a divorce because of legal costs.

The bus passed two kudzu-smothered silos, some gray casino-worker housing, and an old diner known for its fried pickles. Then they entered the gates of a gleaming city with white-hot pavement and pastel buildings. When the bus stopped, the passengers split like a cluster of coins banged out of a paper roll and disappeared into the row of casinos. Liz walked fast, ignoring Peyton, who loped along behind her. In the Western-frontier casino that she preferred, Liz marched straight to the bank. When she left the window with her bucket of nickels, she glimpsed Peyton in the lobby atrium, lounging on a bench near a tree decorated with tiny lights. He followed her to a Vacation USA game, where— one by one—she inserted the ten dollars' worth of nickels included with her bus excursion ticket. She liked to hurry through the first action, just for a little warm-up, as if to prove she could withstand loss.

"Don't mess with my luck, Peyton," she said. "I'm warning you."

Nearby, a woman jerked a machine's arm and a cascade of coins jingled out. "Hey, Mississippi!" the woman cried. "Tunica is where I get lucky. I get nihilistic when I'm in Vegas, but in Tunica I'm flying."

Liz loved coming to Tunica. It was as close to a luxury resort as she would ever get—a bright, clean place where she could feel classy. She delighted in the extravagant newness of the decor. The little lights on the surprisingly non-fake ficus trees in the atrium provided a Christmasy mood. And she loved the incessant sounds of the slots—the boiling of overlapping tones, something like the tune in *Close Encounters of the Third Kind* played by a full-blown orchestra, complete with flashing lights. The Western motif, with boots, guns, and wagon wheels imprinted on the carpeting, was homey. She pictured herself—wisecracking and flamboyant—in a flouncy skirt and boots with spurs.

But today as she wandered through the place, getting her bearings, Peyton trailed her like a hunter, disturbing her concentration. After the first mad rush, she liked to go slowly. Sometimes she preferred to stand in a line for a while, to slow herself down. She liked the suspense of the games—the way they seemed like life-and-death struggles while they were happening. She couldn't bear uncertainty in everyday life, but at the casinos the sudden emotional turns were like a car chase in the movies. The random surprises of playing the slots made her feel she could revamp her life. At times, being married to Peyton was just sitting in chairs compared with this exhilaration. But at other times, being married to him was more volatile and frightening than any gambling action. It was like being knocked backwards by a thug bursting through a door.

A girl in a skimpy black satin-and-lace costume offered her a free rum Coke from a tray. She looked too young for the job, Liz thought. She wore a black knee brace, which seemed to complement her outfit. "Rollerblading?" the server-girl explained in a nasal accent. Peyton was playing a slot next to Liz. As he pulled the arm, a memory flashed through her mind—Peyton grabbing the handle of the fuse box in the basement after a fuse blew. She had been ironing and making toast while he was watching his tape of *Die Hard with a Vengeance*. He often replayed the most violent scenes in his favorite movies. He had a Top Ten list of best wipe-out scenes. "How can you watch all that?" she had asked him. "It's not *my* life," he said with a satisfied smile. "No skin off my butt." She wondered increasingly if she should be afraid, although in his obsession he ignored her, as if he was some-where in the movie and she didn't exist. But now he was stalking her. She wondered if she had been making excuses for him unconsciously. He had his good side—the way he cooked pancakes on Sundays, his habit of making up funny songs to amuse her. She didn't draw conclusions easily about people. But even before he went to jail, her friends had said: Dump him. You'll end up shooting him. Or he'll shoot you. The rum was opening up her head, and she imagined that she was having deep thoughts.

In the afternoon Liz drank another rum Coke, and her luck improved. As she collected a fanfare of coins from a ma-chine's maw, Peyton appeared with a sack of barbecue and Cokes. Carrying her coin bucket, she followed him outside into the hazy, muggy air. They crossed a small bridge to a bench by the brook—the moat that ostensibly allowed the casino to float. Liz thought of the sump pump in her base-ment. When it rained, water seeped in, and the basement smelled like a drainage ditch.

"I'm moving up to the Double Jackpot Haywire," Liz said. "I'm going to put in fifty bucks all at once—in quarters—and then I'm going to hit the MAX button until it gives me back something good."

Her head buzzed. She had forgotten about her stitches, and when she ran her hand through her hair she almost yanked out a stitch, thinking it was a tick.

Peyton handed her a sandwich. She stared at it while he

peeled a straw and stuck it in one of the Cokes for her. They sat on the bench and gazed at the picturesque stream, choked with blooming lilies. Peyton was unusually quiet.

"Why don't you call and find out how your mother is?" Liz said.

"I'll know sooner or later. There's nothing I can do, anyway."

Liz felt a new wave of grief for Daisy—poor, fat Daisy with her mannish cigarette voice and absurd pink pantsuits. Liz had never really liked her. Daisy always told Liz she had no style. Liz meant to find her style one day. It was one of her recent resolutions. Squinting at the sun, Liz blinked the image of Daisy from her mind.

"I thought up a poem for you while I was watching you this morning," Peyton said.

> *"When I count up the stuff I really like,*
> *The first thing for sure is my Harley bike*
> *But I guess that isn't really true*
> *'Cause the thing I really like best is you."*

She held up two fingers. "When I married you, I was about two poker chips short of insanely happy," she said.

"The trouble with you is, you want people to be perfect."

"What do *you* want?" she asked him.

"I want you to stop acting so ill towards me. It makes you ugly."

"Well, leave me alone. Why don't you go over to the Hollywood or Harrah's and leave me here? This is *my* casino." She wadded up her sandwich wrapper. "Hey, what do you mean ugly—looks or acts?"

"I meant your frame of mind makes you act ugly, but I can see it in your face, too. It makes all them little blond hairs stand out and your freckles act like they're on speed." His face lit up in a sort of Bruce Willis sneer, and she knew he was teasing. She had missed that.

She rubbed at her cheek, as if to calm down her freckles. "Are you ashamed of me?"

"For how ugly you act?"

"Oh, shut up." She punched his arm.

"I can't help my mama, but maybe I can help you."

"No, you'd go off and leave me if I was sick. I can't depend on you."

"The reason people stay married is so they can help each other," he said.

"Bullshit," she said.

"I'll help you fix your hair."

"What's wrong with my hair?"

He tousled the top of her head. "It needs a more natural look," he said.

"Watch out—you'll pull my stitches!"

"I hate it that you went and had that operation and I couldn't go with you."

"I don't like you following me around. A girl at work told me I should get a restraining order to stop you from bugging me."

He kicked at the bench. "I've been stupid. If I could roll time back, I wouldn't do a lot of what I done. But it's like that split second when there's a car wreck, and tragedy happens—just like that." He clicked his fingers. "And you can never undo it to save your life. Now Mama might go to her grave with her last picture of me in her mind—Peyton the Jailbird."

His self-pity infuriated her. No tragedy had happened in a split second, she thought.

"To undo the past would be like rolling the Mississippi River backwards," she said.

The little lily-studded brook was sashaying past, but she

had a momentary impression that she was moving, not the water.

During the afternoon she spotted Peyton at a blackjack table. In the past, he typically played till he lost everything; then he always came to her. She'd have five-dollar bills hidden in her clothes in several places—in her inner pockets, in her bra, in a secret pocket fashioned from a drawstring tobacco pouch that she pinned inside her jeans. But he would come after her.

Vaguely aware that he was still parked at the blackjack table, she breezed down the row of slot machines like someone driving a car while mentally miles away. She wasn't focusing on her strategy. She was feeding the machines and drinking rum Cokes. She won ten dollars' worth of quarters on the Triple Diamond and let it ride. It used to be fun to come with Peyton to Tunica. He got her a fake I.D., and they drove down and played until they couldn't stay awake; then they slept in the car at a roadside rest stop, daring criminals and perverts from Highway 61 to kill them—or kidnap them. But that seemed long ago now. She remembered the day he strolled into the backyard and blew apart a rotten stump with some kind of plastic machine pistol. "You can squeeze off a clip in no time flat," he told her later, as if merely mentioning how many screws it took to assemble a patio bench.

Liz pulled the handle and coins rushed out. As long as she stayed lucky, she felt unafraid and rejuvenated, confident she could handle Peyton. He was still engrossed in the blackjack game. His mother's condition had thrown them onto a Tilt-A-Whirl ride, where they spun around separately, sometimes facing each other momentarily before spinning away again. Liz didn't want Daisy to die, and she knew she shouldn't have run away to Tunica. Now she imagined that when she got home, purged of her need to gamble, she could face Daisy's helpless body—maybe even talk her out of her coma. But what she would do about Peyton was a question that trembled in the air like a tossed coin. She knew she had to be resolute. She had been tangled up in the mess of his mind too long. After another spill of quarters from the Triple Diamond, she felt cocky and clear. She would go home, visit Daisy, possibly go to her funeral, then get a restraining order against Peyton. And file for divorce. She tripped over her coin bucket and almost fell into the arms of a leering greaseball with a toothpick in his mouth.

"Come to Daddy!" the guy cried, giving her a hug.

"Fuck off," Liz said, jerking free.

Toward the end of the night Liz was twenty dollars ahead, but in the last hour Peyton begged all her winnings from her for blackjack. He was on a streak, he said. When she relented, he said, "You need me. We're in this together." He stared at her. "I mean that in more ways than one." She told him she wouldn't have let him have her money if his mother wasn't in a coma.

The bus was jammed with jubilant winners laughing and joking, celebrating, and glum losers who stared at their laps. A merry elderly woman across the aisle from Liz and Peyton chattered about the hundred dollars she had won—enough to buy a chimnea, one of those little patio stoves, she announced. Liz's head was about to blow up, and her mind was flying like microwaves blasting from a cell tower. She touched one of her stitches, a little pair of bristles like whiskers. She aimed peppermint breath-killer at her open mouth.

"Sometimes I win and sometimes I lose," said the woman across the aisle. "I started with church bingo and worked my way up. Bingo got me hooked. But I know when to quit."

Peyton nodded. "Everybody's just trying to get a little something, find a way out."

"That's the truth."

"Yessir," Peyton said. "I was in jail, but I never done a thing wrong, and now my poor mama lays dying in a hospital and her last image of me is her son, the jailbird."

The church woman said, "My husband died last year on June twenty-ninth. Cancer. It had spread to his liver. He couldn't pass water, and he was in such pain I was glad to finally see him go. He's home now, with Jesus."

"What?" said Liz, jolted into reality. She might have passed out for a second and missed something. Then she realized it was typical of Peyton to cover his losses by acting unusually sociable. She could sense a hollowness beneath his cheer; he had lost Liz's money, and he was losing his mother. She was tired and didn't want to think.

"You'd make a good preacher," the church woman said to Peyton with a giggle.

"Amen," Liz said, her eye on Peyton.

He said, "Amen, Brother Ben. Shot a goose and killed a hen."

The bus darkened, and the passengers quieted. Some time passed, while Liz sipped from a can of Mountain Dew she had brought on board. All the alcohol she had had earlier that day made her feel chilled, and she removed the fleece throw from her bag and spread it over her bare legs. Peyton was asleep, snoring a little. After a while, a murmur on the bus rose to a loud question.

"This bus is lost," someone said. "Where's he think he's going?"

Liz realized they were journeying on narrow roads through bottomland, not on the four-lane. Thick fog breathed at the windows. She touched Peyton's arm. "We're lost," she whispered. "We're in the Twilight Zone."

"Looks like we might drive right into the river," Peyton said after a bit. He rubbed the sleep from his eyes.

"I don't care if we go to Timbuktu," Liz said. "Where is Timbuktu, anyway?"

"No idea."

"It must be somewhere." Liz tapped the man in front of her on the shoulder. He had a short beard like Peyton used to have. "Do you know where Timbuktu is?"

"Over yonder somewhere," he said, pointing with his elbow. "Over the big pond."

"Wouldn't that be something?" Liz said to the man. "To be hijacked to Timbuktu and nobody knows where it is or how to get there—including the hijacker!" She laughed. "It'll take us a month to get there."

Laughter traveled through the bus. Liz's remarks got passed around, and a couple of passengers began goading the driver to go to Timbuktu.

"This *is* Timbuktu, I believe," someone called out to the driver. "You've hauled us all the way to Timbuktu."

"The old geezers look scared," Peyton said to Liz.

They seemed to be driving over water, but they couldn't see a bridge.

"Hey, don't he have a map?" someone asked.

"We're crossing the Big Muddy," Peyton said.

The invisible bridge was long, and the river a void. The bus hushed.

"Sorry, folks, I dropped the reins back there," the driver eventually admitted over his microphone. He turned on the overhead lights. "Don't worry, we'll get you home. Just hold your horses and I'll figure out what road this is. And it won't go to Timbuktu."

There was a burst of laughter and a little applause.

"I don't believe such a place exists," said the church woman. "It's just a notion, like Never-Never Land."

"Like heaven?" Liz said.

"No. Not at all like heaven. Heaven is a real place. It has gold streets and pearly gates."

"And singing," said Peyton.

"Everybody sings there, whether they can carry a tune or not," said the church woman with a smile. "Law', I hate to sing. I purely dread heaven."

"Do you dread heaven, Liz?" asked Peyton as the lights dimmed again.

"No. Heaven's the least of my worries."

The bus quieted. Most of the passengers seemed to nod off. After awhile, Peyton slipped his hand under the fleece throw on Liz's lap. His hand rested between her thighs like a sleeping cat. It lay there, its dark heat firing her. Then, under the blanket, his hand began undulating slowly up her leg, inside her shorts. She sat up straight, wide awake, and stared out at the fog. She inched her legs apart. And before long he was finger-fucking her hard, then smoothly, expertly. She felt the peacefulness of giving in, the delicious limbo of temptation, where everything at stake seemed make-believe. For the time being, she was waiting for the spinning images of her life to line up in a perfect row.

Thunder Snow

Boogie tried to talk Darlene into staying home that weekend—heavy snow was predicted—but she wouldn't listen. She had volunteered to drive up to Cincinnati to retrieve her cousin Fentress's thyroid medicine and then carry it to her all the way down in Bell County.

"I don't want you going down there into those mountains if it gets bad."

"I'll be on four-lanes most of the way," she said. "If I can't get through to Pineville, I'll just stop at Aunt Gladys's house. Don't worry, Boogie. I'll watch out. You worry too much."

Boogie did worry about Darlene. Their separation during the Gulf War had been traumatic for him, causing him to become overly protective. He had been terrified that she would return from Saudi Arabia in a body bag. For a woman to come home from a war that way was an intolerable notion.

But she shrugged off both the terror and the glamour of the war—a lot of sand and bad food and heavy work loading vehicles, she said. "Somebody had to kick Saddam's butt," she said when she got home. For a time, she marched around the house like a stranger. He noticed how the permanent in her hair had grown out.

The sky was clear when Darlene headed for Cincinnati on Sunday morning. She would visit her mother, collect the medicine Fentress had accidentally left there, then head for Pineville on Monday. On Sunday evening rain began falling. It turned to sleet. Later, during the night, Boogie could sense the silence of snow over the house and yard. In the morning he lay still in bed for a few moments. He heard no traffic, no planes, no dogs or birds. He got up and pulled the drapes apart. The snow was coming down in thick blobs fat as cotton balls. Already it had covered the barbecue grill on the porch, and the bushes out back appeared to be a row of snow soldiers.

He telephoned Darlene's mother.

"She left two hours ago," Loretta said. "She thought she could beat it, but it commenced to snowing about an hour ago."

"It's snowing here," Boogie said. "She'll be driving right into it."

"I imagine she'll head home and not try to go down to Fentress's till tomorrow," Loretta said. She coughed loudly. "Lord, I'm strangled. Darlene had to go to the all-night place and bring me some cough syrup."

Loretta worked at a dry cleaner's, and in the winter the fumes made her throat raw.

Boogie said, "If Darlene comes back, or calls, tell her to stop somewhere and not try to drive in the snow. Tell her I said so."

Loretta said, "Well, I don't know what she's aiming to

do. Fentress don't have to have her medicine till Thursday."
She stopped to cough. "I told Darlene I didn't think Fentress ought to keep on taking something that's radioactive.
They're probably doing some kind of experiment on her."

"It's not radioactive," Boogie said.

"I know you and Darlene keep saying that, but I believe it
is. Darlene's real good to traipse up here and fetch it for her,
though."

"She likes to drive," Boogie said. "That's what it is."

"She said she'd carry me down to Pine Mountain for
Easter, but I told her she needn't."

Boogie shoveled out the driveway, angry at himself for not
driving Darlene to Cincinnati. But he had been on the weekend shift. Surely she wouldn't try to drive to Pineville in
the snow, he thought. She had been born in the Kentucky
mountains but had grown up in Cincinnati, where her parents had moved after her father lost his job in the mines.
Darlene said they had worn a path back home to Pine Mountain, they went back to visit so often.

At work, half of the machines were down. Boogie's team
was short two workers, and they had to rejigger the controls
of the main machine, which directed the manufacture of
some small plastic computer-casing parts. Boogie filled out
the paperwork and checked on the timing of his number-three stamper. Some wheels were spinning in front of him.
He reset a dial. He felt like a pilot in a cockpit. He often
imagined he was flying. He could see himself in a Strike
Eagle, swooping and plunging like a mighty bird.

"I had to walk half a mile to feed our neighbor's cows,"
said Beverly Cox, from her computer station. "I thought my
toes were frostbit."

"Why didn't your husband go feed the cows instead of
you?" Boogie asked. He would have done that for Darlene.
He would have insisted.

"Cows ain't his thing," Beverly said. "If it don't eat regular unleaded, he don't want it. He don't even want a dog."

One of the managers stepped out of a connecting tunnel. "Traffic's backed up on I-75 south," he said, gleeful with his news. "The trucks can't get over Jellico Mountain. The governor's talking about closing down the interstates."

At break, Boogie went to the pay phone, but a dozen people were in line and nobody was getting through. The circuits were busy.

"I don't see how folks up north put up with weather like this," said a wide-bodied guy Boogie knew as Big George.

"Snow—they can have it, I hate it," said Beverly as she ripped open a candy bar.

"Darlene loves it," Boogie said. "I bet she's having a big time out there while I sit around and worry."

"Darlene needs a car phone," said Beverly.

"That's what I want for Christmas," said Big George.

"They cost a fortune," Boogie said.

"What's a fortune if it saves your life?" Beverly sent her candy wrapper flying. "I told Ken if he didn't get me one he might find me in a ditch in pieces."

"Darlene always thinks she can do anything," Boogie said, wincing. "She'll drive and drive till she gets stuck. I know *her*."

"Oh, she'll probably stop somewhere and call," Beverly said in a sympathetic tone that made Boogie feel even worse.

At six o'clock, soon after Boogie got home, his National Guard unit called him out for the snow emergency. The weather service said this was the worst winter storm in over fifteen years. Garbed in layers, he struggled into the blowing snow. As he drove to the armory, he passed several ditched cars, and he skidded a couple of times himself. The trees had been coated with ice yesterday, and now the snow hung on in great clumps, bending the boughs low. He wondered where the birds were. The radio said it was going down to zero; already the wind-chill factor was five below.

He hadn't heard from her. He'd found only one message on his answering machine, from Darlene's brother Jack. "Boogie, how's the storm treating you? Are you O.K.? Got enough supplies? Did Darlene get back from Cincinnati? I hope she didn't head down to Pineville with Fentress's medicine."

Snow made hats on garbage cans. Boogie saw a doghouse blown full of snow. He thought for a moment about Alexander, how he used to love to play in the snow. They had had to put him to sleep last winter. Freezing to death would be like being put to sleep. They said freezing in the snow was like drifting away under a soft blanket. You felt like you were settling in for a long winter's nap. Once your mind froze, you couldn't keep on fighting, he thought with a shudder.

Her funeral wouldn't be here, he thought, or even in Cincinnati. It would be in Bell County, with all her kinfolks. He always planned her funeral when he was worried that she'd had a wreck. Sometimes he worried so much that he got pissed when she showed up safely. When she left for Saudi Arabia, he had said, "You better come back. I don't want to have to listen to all your kinfolks wailing and weeping at your funeral." And she said, "They'll just cry long enough to get it out of their system and then they'll try to sue the government and then they'll forget all about me." She had grinned so big when she said that.

Gusts of snow blew in front of the car as he felt his way toward Man o' War Boulevard. He was creeping past a horse farm. The snow-covered fields made him think of the desert. Black fences rimmed with snow created a grid against the blank, vanished ground. He saw five snow-blanketed horses huddled under a clump of trees. He wondered if they were

Arabian horses. He was surprised they weren't lolling on feather beds in their climate-controlled barns. Racehorses got better care than some people, he thought. Gazing at the broad plain of horse pastures, he thought about Darlene's people shut up in those close, tight little mountains. Darlene had said it used to snow at her grandparents' place on Pine Mountain more than it ever snowed in Lexington. The closeness of the mountains held the cold air longer and drew more snow in, she said. Darlene was always saying, "I wish it would come a sixteen-footer."

"Sixteen Tons." Song he remembered from the oldies station. The radio now was listing cancellations. Self-help groups, church groups, schools, a basketball game. The snow glistened and gleamed in the night. His car seemed to be crunching and swaying through heavy sand. "Did you miss it here?" he had asked her when she came back from the war. "Did you think about me?"

"We were too busy to think," she said. "It was another world."

Now the radio was saying the weather was worse than the storm of 'seventy-eight. The wind-chill was going down to minus fifteen. A truck in front of him was weaving. Boogie took his foot off the gas. The truck ahead straightened out.

When he met Darlene, he had just moved to Lexington from the flat western end of the state and was living in a rooming house until he could get his bearings. By the time he did, he and Darlene were talking about how many children they wanted. After five years, they were still childless, and they were not sure why she couldn't get pregnant. Sometimes it seemed that she held herself separate from him so that there was an essential part of her he could never reach. He wished they could act like kids again together. He wanted to boogie in the snow with her.

Boogie got his nickname when he was just a toddler, dancing to his mother's old fifties records. Everybody found his little dance amusing. He was petted, an only boy in a houseful of girls. His nickname had always embarrassed him, but Darlene loved it. Not long ago, they saw Little Richard on TV entertaining the President at some Washington thing. Little Richard, in a black suit with sequined sleeves and gold buttons and braid, was screaming out the gospel like he'd just invented it. Darlene said, "How can President Bill just set there like a knot on a log and not get up and boogie?"

At the airport, Boogie followed a trail to the armory, where he was flagged in. Several small airplanes on the tarmac resembled seabirds, snowbound and frozen to the beach. Two large aircraft—a DC-9 and one of those windowless horse-transport planes—stirred his desire to fly. He should have been a pilot, he thought. But that hadn't occurred to him when he dropped out of college.

He stopped at a gate and rolled down his window.

"Hey, we're going out in the Humvees!" a heavy man in an orange deer-hunting suit said to him. "Why, you're Boogie Jones. I knew your wife at Fort Campbell." The guy laughed apologetically. "I didn't mean that the way it sounded." A drop of clear liquid was poised on the end of his nose. "I'm liable to get myself in trouble," he said with a muffled guffaw.

"Point the way," Boogie said.

"It's going down below zero tonight," the man in the orange suit said. "That wind-chill factor is what makes it so cold. It's going to be twenty below wind-chill."

He directed Boogie to a plowed-out parking area. Boogie skidded into the spot a little too fast, jumping the brakes too hard. It made him angry to think of guys like that out on maneuvers with Darlene. Or in some godforsaken desert half the world away. Boogie had parked too close to a van and couldn't get his door open, so he had to start the engine again and back up. He knew the kind of stuff that went on in wartime, but when Darlene was over there he had tried not to think about it. Instead, he had followed the maps on television, the movements of the Humvees through the shifting, whispering sands. Line from some poem? He followed the air war, then the tanks. She wouldn't have been in a plane or a tank. She would have been in a tent or a barracks. He knew perfectly well the unspoken reality of war: It was a sexual high; so far away from home, in the face of death, anything was O.K. In fact, when she was gone, he sort of got to know Dottie Henderson next door. Her brother was over in Saudi flying Warthogs. Dottie had CNN on all the time and taped the other news programs. She had three TVs and three VCRs. Whenever a Warthog went down, Boogie went over and waited with her to find out whose plane it was. She gave him food she was always apologizing for. But she was far too old for him, and she had old-fashioned women's interests, such as theme luncheons. Her garden luncheon featured dirt cakes—chocolate cakes baked in flowerpots and decorated with Gummi Worms.

Boogie's partner for this evening was Glenn Forrest, an insurance salesman. "These Hummers are little tanks in jeep clothing," Glenn said, patting the low top of the vehicle almost affectionately. Boogie grunted.

Behind the wheel of the Humvee, Boogie set forth on his night mission. It was his turn in the combat zone, he thought. In the war, her unit was called up and his wasn't, and now, in the snow, *he* was on duty. But again they were apart.

In a Humvee, he could practically fly through the drifts. He wheeled around the airport, crunching through a foot and a half of virgin snow, then headed out to one of the subdivisions to pick up a surgeon who had to get to the university hospital. The doctor said he had surgery scheduled in the morning. "It won't happen," he said as he got in the back seat. He was carrying a gym bag and wearing jeans and a Wildcats jacket.

"What kind of surgery?" Glenn asked the doctor.

"Just a splenectomy. It'll probably be rescheduled."

"My wife had her appendix out," Glenn said. "She almost died because they waited so long to go in. They thought she had food poisoning."

Boogie said, "My wife and I went to the clinic there last summer." He hesitated, wondering whether to ask this doctor's opinion. Then he blurted out all about the fertility tests he and Darlene had taken.

"My sperm count was over ninety million," Boogie said. "They told me that was great."

"Wow," Glenn said. He took off a glove and blew on his fingers.

"That's good," the doctor said, leaning forward from the back. "What did your wife's test show?"

"They said there wasn't anything they could find that was keeping her from getting pregnant. Just takes time, I reckon." Boogie glanced back at the doctor. "Wouldn't you think if you shot off ninety million bullets at once, one of 'em would hit the target? And that's ninety million in about one drop. There's billions!"

"Depends on your aim!" said Glenn with an explosion of laughter.

Boogie wanted to ask the doctor whether something could have happened to Darlene in the Gulf War to cause her infertility, but he lost his nerve. The doctor thanked him for the ride when he got out.

As Boogie fooled with the windshield wiper knob, Glenn said, "This is the kind of night that makes you think it's time for Jesus to show up again. Don't it look like the end of the world? If Jesus was to come back here right in the middle of this snowstorm, boy would he be mad! He'd start making a list. First, he'd want to know why families ain't at home together of a night and why all the children's carrying guns to school. And then he'd go through all the murders and sex crimes. And he'd want to know why there's not enough snowplows in Kentucky."

"I imagine," Boogie said. He let Glenn continue with Jesus' list while he concentrated on his driving. There was so much crazy talk going on these days anyway, Boogie just let it swirl. The shifting, whispering sands kept drifting through his head.

He had a job to do. As he smashed through snowbanks, he pretended he was piloting an F-14, the Tomcat. He carried Phoenix and Sparrow and Sidewinder missiles. Birds and snakes. He was on combat air-patrol loiter time, he figured, waiting for the action. From the TV news, he had learned all the aircraft over there. The snowed-over DC-9 at the airport had twin engines on the sides like the A-10 Warthog. The Warthog was the ugliest plane ever built, yet it could pirouette. It could waltz and swing. It could probably even boogie. It had a cannon protruding from its nose that was powerful enough to kill a tank or a Scud launcher. It would fly in low, and so slowly that its tight moves were beautiful.

Back then, when Darlene was over there, he found out that the letters in THE PERSIAN GULF could be rearranged to spell U.S. FIGHTER PLANE. For months, he kept thinking there was surely some significance in that.

All evening, Boogie was busy saving lives. He ferried some nurses to Good Sam Hospital, on Limestone, and transported a woman to the emergency room after she had fallen on ice. The ambulances were slipping and sliding, too. He called the state police to see if he could get word about Darlene. They said traffic on I-75 was backed up for thirty miles. The governor had closed the interstates.

"I could drive this thing right on out to I-75 and find her," Boogie said to Glenn.

"The cops don't want us out there."

"They probably couldn't catch us in this. We'd hum right up the median."

Glenn lit a cigarette and blew out clouds. He said, "I bet them rigs stuck on I-75 are mad as hell."

Boogie nodded. Ernie, the truck dispatcher at the plant, would be full of tales of truckers trying to get their shipments through the mountains south of Lexington.

A stranded motorist cussed at Boogie for refusing to drive him to the mall. "Sorry, buddy," Boogie said with a wave. "Hospitals have priority."

At one of their stops, a nurse handed them slices of pizza and paper cups of coffee. Gratefully, they gulped the hot food. Boogie felt warmer. He wondered if Jesus would like pizza. A moment before, Glenn had pronounced Jesus a Republican. Glenn was a one-man talk show.

Boogie's toes felt frozen. He couldn't seem to get any heat from the engine. The Humvee was canvas-topped, so the cold came right in. On the desert, it would have been the heat. Darlene had told him it was so hot she thought she'd die. She got an infected sunburn, despite precautions. It was so dark in Desert Storm, he thought as he headed out Nicholasville to Man o' War. He recalled his fear the night the ground war began. The vision of all those tanks rumbling along seemed even darker and more hazardous than the air war. When planes like the Tomcat and the Strike Eagle took off at night, you could see a dim silhouette on the runway, in the blackness, but mainly all you saw were blinking lights and long plumes of blue-white flame bursting from the afterburners. In combat, the afterburners would glow again.

Now he felt his afterburners charge. He imagined fireworks and speed.

He turned down a side street. A snowplow had created a bank of snow at the entrance to the next street. He busted effortlessly through the three-foot dune.

"Hot damn!" cried Glenn. "My little boys would sure love this."

When they arrived back at the armory, a news team was on the scene, its familiar van topped with a satellite dish like a huge suction cup. An attractive woman was waving a microphone at him. She was standing by a snowbank. He recognized her face from the evening news—gorgeous Shelley Collins. He hadn't realized she would be so tall. She was tall like a camel.

"Could I talk with you a moment, sir? We're live on camera."

Carefully, Boogie picked his way through the snow toward the woman. He didn't want to fall on television. He shivered with cold.

"What's your name?" she asked. She didn't even have a hat on. Her glowing blond hair was round like a helmet. Snowflakes buzzed around her face like moths.

"Boogie Jones," he said. "William Jones, actually, but everybody calls me Boogie." Did he have to explain this? He felt embarrassed. Who would care what his name was or even whether he was embarrassed?

"Well, Boogie, I see that you have been helping to get some emergency errands done. Can you tell us a little about what it's like to ride around in one of these Humvees that we see behind us here?"

"Well, they're powerful machines," Boogie said, stomping the numbness from one foot. "You can drive 'em anywhere. The Humvee can go just about anywhere you want it to go except straight up." He laughed. "It would put a billy goat to shame."

"And how warm is it inside there? Pretty chilly?"

Boogie laughed again. He could imagine sailing easily into the deep waters of flirtation. He said, "It's got a manifold heater, meaning the heat comes off the engine? And it ain't much. It's about like having a dog breathe on your boots."

He was about to add that he was looking for his wife, that she was lost in the snow, but Shelley Collins thanked him briskly and said, "Now, back to you, Murray."

Ten minutes later, inside the armory, as Boogie hovered over a radiator trying to get thawed out, a state policeman came in calling, "William Jones. William Jones." Boogie jumped.

"Got word from your wife," the officer said with a smile. "She saw you on television and got a cop to radio in. She said to tell you she's fine."

Darlene didn't get home until early Wednesday, when the interstates opened. She had been stranded north of Lexington and hadn't gone to Pineville. She came in chattering and complaining that her hair was dirty. She went to fill the bird feeder first thing and saw that he had filled it. She seemed edgy and impatient. It was sort of fun, she told him after she had made some coffee. She had been holed up with about fifty people—mostly truckers—in a motel lobby. The motel let them have cots and bedding.

He gazed at her, his wife, imagining her sleeping in a motel lobby with a bunch of truckers. Or in the desert with an army. They had never really discussed what she might have done in Saudi Arabia. Whenever he brought it up, she snapped something about trust. He recalled her words when he met her at the airport on her return. All smiles, she had said, "There's my rootin', tootin', boot-scootin' Boogie!"

"There were some little kids at the motel," she said now, handing him a mug of coffee. "Their parents were bored stiff, but the kids were so full of life. I made a snowman with a couple of little boys. One of the kids was named Shane and the other one was Jade. I told them a story about the Great Snowman. I told them to make a wish and the Great Snowman would bring them something nice. Their daddy watched me like a hawk. You can't even carry on a conversation with a child these days without everybody jumping on you."

She began to sob. A rigor surged up Boogie's spine, like a snake swishing. He grasped her and held her tight, as if he were catching her as she was falling.

"I was so worried about you," he said, his face brushing her ponytail. Her hair was oily and smelled of tobacco.

"I couldn't get word to you," she said. "I should have stayed with Mama."

"It was strange," he said. "When you were over there in the war, I kept looking for you on television and never could find you. And this time you found me on television."

She stopped crying. "I had a dream about the war," she said, breaking away from him. "I thought I was in the barracks again. For a second, I thought a Scud had hit."

She sat down on the couch. He moved aside a pillow and sat close to her, putting his arm around her. She squirmed.

"It was just the snowstorm," she said. "There was lightning, and the thunder woke me up. I couldn't believe it was thunder. How could it be thunder?"

"It was thunder snow," Boogie said soothingly. "When you have lightning and thunder in a snowstorm, they call it thunder snow."

"I thought it was old So-Damn Insane after me." She laughed and blew her nose.

"No, old Saddam won't ever get you, not if I can help it," said Boogie, grinning.

He remembered the fireworks over Baghdad, the dark sky above Kuwait, the black oil slick—all the pictures he had seen on television. He didn't know what she had seen over there. It would have been entirely different, he realized. It wouldn't have been those pictures at all.

"I wasn't crying over the war," she said. "I wish you would just forget about that. I wanted to make snow cream with those little boys. I wanted to do that worse than anything. You're not supposed to make it anymore, everything's so dirty, but that new snow looked so pure. I haven't had snow cream in forever."

"I bet we could make some," said Boogie hopefully. "We could dig down and get some clean snow out from underneath."

"I don't think we've got any vanilla," she said.

"We haven't got any milk either," he said, disappointed. "I forgot to get any." For a moment, he felt inadequate, as if the best he could do for her was reassure her that thunder could indeed occur in a snowstorm. But he knew he could do better than that. It struck him that he had to stop hovering over her so much, so a clear avenue would open up between them. *Then* they would have a baby. It had to be this gulf between them that was keeping a family from taking root. He knew it would seem silly if he said that aloud, but there was truth to it, he was sure.

Darlene stood up, shivering, like a tree shedding snow from its branches in the wind. Her hair was pulled back with a ruffle of gauze, a glorified rubber band. Her eyes had slightly blue shadows under them. He stood beside his wife, speechless, as she vibrated with energy.

She said, "As soon as the roads are clear, I'm heading

down to Pineville with Fentress's medicine. I'll have to take off from work again, but she's got to have it by tomorrow night."

What flashed into Boogie's mind was the Tomahawk cruise missile, sailing directly above a Baghdad street, with tiny little fold-up wings like some weird bug's. It cruised along as if it had a mind of its own, and when it reached the corner, it turned left.

Rolling into Atlanta

Each night when Annie got in from work, she watched the late movie on TV and ate a cold boiled egg with a Coca-Cola, sometimes with sesame crackers if she remembered to bring a few packets from the restaurant where she had been a hostess for the past two weeks. She had been drifting off to sleep between one and two, and at five o'clock a loud noise somewhere in the building always woke her briefly and made her visualize a door slamming on her past. That she translated every sensation into metaphor nowadays was perfectly appropriate, she thought.

She was staying in a rent-free condo. The owner, a lawyer named Clayton Scoville, was white-water rafting on the Zambezi. She had never met him and didn't know what he looked like. There were no photographs in the place, just undistinguished oil reproductions (a mountain, a waterfall, birds in flight). She wasn't used to such luxury—Mexican-style tile, curvilinear cabinets, halogen lighting, bottomless carpet, two bathrooms. Red parrots cavorted in the emerald jungle print on the shower curtains. The lawyer used black bath soap, bright green towels. He subscribed to *Outside* and *Time* and *Smart Money*. A closet was crammed with sporting goods, mostly items that didn't seem to belong here in Atlanta—ice skates, skis, ski clothing, a fur-lined cap with fold-down earflaps. She imagined he was a person who could pick up and leave, a person like her. She had arrived with two suitcases and within hours had bought a second-hand Honda Civic that had been repossessed by a finance company. In the car's trunk were a pair of baggy-style shorts and a matching loud-pink floral shirt—size ten, too large for Annie—and a tattered copy of *Freaky Deaky*.

Tonight a fund-raising pledge drive on the public television station had delayed the late movie, so Annie turned on the classic-rock radio station she listened to in the mornings. The Rolling Stones were coming to Atlanta later in the month, and the station was sponsoring a contest for free tickets. The D.J.s urged listeners to construct and decorate a box, no larger than seven by four by three, to live in for twenty-four hours, in isolation. The best three boxes would be set up in a corner of the studio. Annie had been hearing Stones music all week, and its raunchy urgency made her feel important things were happening in this city. She liked Atlanta—its clean, busy beauty. She opened the sliding doors to the sundeck and finished her Coke out there. The deck— with a tub of gardenias, a cherry-tomato plant, and a clematis climbing a trellis—opened out into a cozy, fenced yard. It was a mild autumn night, and the lights over at the shopping center silhouetted the feathery palm trees outside the nearby T.G.I. Friday's. The sound of the radio spilled out like light into the dim parking lot.

Annie was a sort of undercover agent. She had been hostessing at a Chez Suzanne's in Texas and had met one of the executives, Andrew Parrell, from the New Orleans corporate headquarters. She had drinks with him a couple of times, and he hired her to seek out irregularities at the chain's Atlanta restaurant. He even found her this place to stay—Clayton Scoville was an old friend of his. So that the Atlanta management wouldn't suspect, she had to interview for the job, which she got on the spot. Andrew wanted her just to observe, to find out if anything funny was going on. He suspected stealing. She wrote detailed daily reports on staff morale and telephoned Andrew every two or three days.

Annie Rhodes, Girl P.I. It sounded like one of the juvenile mysteries she used to read. It had a nice ring to it. And she'd earn more money than before—even more if she got to switch to cocktailing. Andrew wanted her to stay a month or two, and then he would send her to another restaurant. She hadn't minded leaving Texas, a place she didn't really know anyway. It was just the place she landed after college. Most of her college friends had spread out, and a few of them were in the Southeast, so she jumped at the chance to come here.

"Just be yourself," Andrew said reassuringly. "And don't get personally involved."

She was herself, for the most part. The lie was the guy she'd moved here to be near. Andrew said she had to have a cover. So she invented Scott. He was six feet tall, a runner, and he had dark hair with a little kink to it. His work had something to do with computers. He traveled the South, coming to Atlanta frequently on jobs that were vague in her mind, but she hit on some realistic touches about him. His mother was a Catholic and his father a Protestant; they ran a grocery in Ypsilanti, Michigan. Scott had a retarded sister in an institution. He broke his leg once playing football. Annie had met him at school, where he had a computer-science scholarship that paid for everything but his books. His grandmother paid for his books, Annie figured.

Annie, the Spy. So far, she hadn't noticed anything unusual. The caramel drops on the meringue dessert; the food inspectors hanging around a long time one evening, buddy-buddies with the manager; the waitress who had once worked for the Carter family when Jimmy Carter was in the statehouse—"A cold fish if you ever saw one," she said, and shivered.

Annie's hostess smile was efficient and convincing. She had heard that keeping up such an act made that sort of job among the world's most stressful, but she didn't mind. It was like being on automatic pilot. Occasionally, a man tried to slip her a five for a good table. But that was against policy. Tonight she noticed that the ficus tree in the foyer was remarkably dusty and sticky. Its leaves gave off a gummy substance that had dripped to the floor. In the mellow, atmospheric lighting the splotches were hardly noticeable, but her senses seemed sharpened now. She felt incredibly observant. She noticed the small ways the design of the abstract beige-and-blue decor varied from that at the sister restaurant. She noticed the supply of maraschino cherries arriving in a stained box that had been taped together; the colored lights that danced in the outdoor fountain at a slightly different speed from the similar fountain lights at the Texas place; the bartender's cold, sad eyes. He had told her he had a daughter in college, a daughter who had frilly hair like hers. He used the word "frilly." He meant permed.

During the pre-dinner lull, she mentioned the sticky ficus to the head waiter, Wes Simmons, a pleasant fellow who seemed to be on good terms with everyone. Wes had a silly manner of joking with the staff, but at the same time Annie detected a genuineness beneath his conventional Southern charm. He was good-looking, in a weird way.

"Why don't they get an artificial tree?" he said, testing his shoe on a sticky spot. "This is ridiculous."

Theresa, a waitress with a modest, outdated punk hairstyle, said, "That tree's got a case of scale." She felt the leaves. "You can't hardly see them. They're little bitty brown bugs that make all that sticky stuff."

"What can I do with it?" said Wes, squinting at the underside of a leaf. "Spray it right here, with all this food?"

"Set it out in the sun for two weeks," advised Theresa. "And repotting helps."

"You can put it on my sundeck," said Annie.

"I'll have to do something," Wes said. He yawned, then apologized. "I was in line since midnight last night to get Stones tickets and then found out they wouldn't take Visa! But this nice lady in line with me offered to let me borrow the cash. Nowadays something like that is so hard to believe, and then I think: Hurray, this is still the Old South." He lifted his shoe again and examined the sole.

"Oh, do you have any extra tickets?" Annie asked. She hadn't even imagined being able to get tickets.

"All I got are spoken for. I wish I could help you out."

"I love the Stones. My sister saw them once in Lexington, but I was too young to go."

"I always say if I could just see the Rolling Stones, I could die happy," Wes said dreamily. He moved into the dining area and straightened a stack of napkins. Casually he twirled a peach-hued napkin into a fan and thrust it into a wineglass. Annie had learned that he had an extensive collection of *Nova* shows on tape and that he used to work for an escort service, but she didn't know what to make of those facts. She wondered if she should have mentioned her sister in Lexington. Maybe she should have made up a brother in Chillicothe, Ohio. She shouldn't have offered her sundeck for the sick plant.

In the kitchen later in the evening, Wes grabbed a croissant and stuffed it with a hunk of chicken.

"My tastes don't run to paté and coq au vin," he said as he squirted ketchup onto his sandwich. "Want to go with me to Uncle Frog's Rib Shack sometime and get some real food?"

"What would my boyfriend say?"

"He'd say I feed you good," he said, teasing. "Sorry I can't take you to see the Stones. I could take you to Stone Mountain. But I guess that would be a dumb substitute."

"Did you mean what you said—that you could die happy if you saw the Rolling Stones?"

"Sometimes I think like that," he said, embarrassed. "I just can't think of anything that would top the Stones, ecstasy-wise."

The way he said "ecstasy-wise" made Annie laugh. He was mocking the restaurant manager's pompous jargon. She liked Wes, but she caught herself, as if there were a child inside her about to slam through a car windshield. What if she fell in love with him? She suddenly felt as though she were in a movie but simultaneously watching it, waiting to see what would happen. That evening at a corner table a pair of lovers were celebrating their engagement. They ordered everything rich, starting with brandy Alexanders and oysters on the half shell and finishing with fluted chocolate cups plopped full of peanut-butter mousse. He gave her the ring during the dessert, just after the champagne was poured. Annie got the impression that the proposal had been a total surprise to the woman. Annie heard her whine, "But I have to study for my CPA exam."

"When are you going to settle down?" Annie's father wanted to know when she called her parents a little later that eve-

ning. She used the pay phone in the corridor by the rest-
rooms and called collect, something her parents still insisted
she do.

"I'm not through rambling yet," she said. "I haven't even
been to California. Or Alaska. I want to go to Alaska and
roam around the tundra someday."

"It's cold in Alaska," he said. "Do you plan to live in an
igloo?"

"Funny, Dad. Very funny."

She didn't tell her parents she was working undercover.
They watched too much television.

Her father said, "I worry about you, honey. Atlanta's a big
city."

"Yes, but it's really very interesting. Everything's called
Peachtree here. Peachtree Street. Peachtree Plaza. It's a real
peachy place."

"I know I can't talk you into getting a handgun, but at
least you need a dog."

The thought of a dog struck her deeply, like what journal-
ists call hard news. She hadn't had a dog in three years. She
didn't mind being alone, and she kept thinking fondly of her
suddenly widowed aunt Helen, who had jaunted off to Europe alone when getting a refund on the trip she'd planned
with her husband proved to be problematic. Aunt Helen had
the adventure of her life. It occurred to Annie that she'd
rather have a dog than the ghostly Scott, who was beginning
to seem like a creep. The notion of Scott had come to her
during the flight to Atlanta, when she read an article about
Japan in an airline magazine. In Japan, there were agencies
that rented people out as wedding guests. It was cheaper to
rent a person to play an old grandmother than to ship the
real one in from the mountains. And people wanted important guests at their weddings, so they rented actors to imper-
sonate public officials. All week Annie had been thinking

about how some people wanted to believe that appearance and reality were the same. Later that evening, she realized that when she said good night to the bartender and told him she was going to see Scott that weekend she had momentarily believed it was true. She drove home from work, imagining Scott as one of those rag-doll dummies frightened women set in their passenger seats to ward off strangers.

"Andrew, I don't have much to report. Agnes went home early with an upset stomach. Frank, the salad man, said his car was being repossessed. One of the busboys flirted with me."

"You're doing fine," said Andrew. "It'll take a while."

"One of the customers insisted he smelled pot in the restroom."

"Write that down. And just keep your eyes open. I always thought the problem there could turn out to be drugs."

"Are you kidding? You didn't mention that." Annie was exasperated with Andrew at times. He assumed too much, and he had such a limited life. All he did besides work was watch *Star Trek* reruns and ESPN. She knew little more about him except that he was stingy and insisted on a first-name basis with Annie, which made her feel peculiar and wary. She was glad she hadn't slept with him those times she went out with him. He was too old, for one thing.

"I'll tell you exactly what to do, and you'll be fully protected," he was saying.

"I don't know if I can handle this."

"Don't worry. You're doing fine."

"You didn't tell me about this before."

"Just act normal. Nobody knows who you are."

She hung up the phone and sped eggshell fragments down the garbage disposal. She turned on her late movie and double-checked the chain on the door. Andrew was in outer space, she thought. She couldn't imagine a serious drug problem at the restaurant. The bar was so relaxed, the clientele upscale, the waiters so correct. She wondered about Boyd and Jim, the rock-and-roll busboys. They belonged to a band called Exact Change Lane. Boyd used to work in Texas, and he had chatted with Annie about how Dallas had changed. Annie hadn't realized it had changed. The only time she was in Dallas there had been a horrible crash on the highway because of the blinding sunset reflections off one of the gold-glass buildings on the outskirts of the city. Boyd and Jim acted a bit haughty because they played in a band, but Annie liked most of the people she worked with. She had gone for drinks with some of the staff a few times after work. They were beer drinkers, except for Yvonne, who liked rusty nails for their sweetness. Yvonne had black Diana Ross hair and wore huge amounts of amethyst jewelry. Annie went out for ice cream with another waitress who confided she was having an affair and her husband didn't suspect. Annie felt like a rat, reporting the woman's secret to Andrew, who wasn't even interested. Everyone asked Annie, "How do you like Atlanta?" and everyone said Atlanta was on the move.

Andrew kept assuring her that the important thing was to keep an open mind. So she reported the times people were tardy; petty complaints and moods; the bartender's mournful commentaries about his wayward daughter. She had to be sharp. Every moment should be like this, she thought, surging inside with a sort of lust for something filling and indefinable—life. The feeling was a little goofy, she thought, so she didn't tell Andrew. And she didn't report Wes's jokes, or the way he smiled when he saw her coming toward him as if he were startled by a pleasant memory. She didn't mention the insect bites on his neck—he had been camping in Oconee National Forest and got drenched in a storm. Annie was struck by such a desire to go camping that she found herself digging into the lawyer's closets for a look at his camping gear.

Comments she overheard among the staff:

"She was water-skiing and her bladder fell out."

"Chicken is on all the diets. It must be low in everything."

"I'm going to get my hide tacked to the wall if I don't get home early."

"Mom always puts my clothes in the destruct cycle of the dryer and they come out doll clothes."

"Did you know you can make lip gloss in a microwave? Mix lipstick with petroleum jelly and zap it on high."

Was there a clue? Something she was missing?

Her weekends were Mondays and Tuesdays. On Monday, she awoke with the five-o'clock boom somewhere in the building, then drifted back into a vague sunlit sleep. She dreamed about Scott, his image as clear as a long-distance voice on the telephone when one says in surprise, "You sound like you're in the next room." Scott had long skinny arms and a face like a terrier, with brown-and-white mottled fur. In the dream it was called pinto fur. She began to wake up. He would have been waiting for her last night, she thought, working out her story about the weekend to tell Wes and the others. While she was out shopping he would catch up on some of his paperwork—on his little laptop in her living room—and then they would go see about getting her a dog. Scott didn't like dogs, though.

Now it was ten o'clock, and the radio was yammering away at her. The Rolling Stones update. "Only days away . . . Build a box . . . Your little home away from home . . . Bring it to our studio and be one of three lucky ones whose boxes are chosen . . . The only rule is you cannot get out for twenty-four hours, so you figure out what luxuries and con-veniences you want in your little mini-condo there. Ha ha.

Come on, you Georgia peaches out there! The Stones are rolling into Atlanta pretty real soon!" The song "Mixed Emotions" drove her fully awake. She felt something urgent calling her from deep within, like a creature who had fallen into a cistern.

The telephone was ringing.

"Annie? It's Wes. Did I wake you up?"

"That's O.K." She turned down the radio.

"Hey, I've got an extra pair of Stones tickets for you. I promised them to my little cousins, Barb and Jan, but now their mama won't let them come all the way from Alabama. They're seventy-five apiece, and you can have them at cost. I wouldn't try to scalp you."

"Oh, I don't know if Scott can go." She felt how sharp she was to remember Scott so quickly, on the spot.

"When can you find out?"

"Oh, I want to go anyway. I'd love to go."

"What about the other ticket?"

"I'll buy both of them," Annie said quickly. "If he can't go, I have an old college friend in Chattanooga. I'm sure Tina would give anything to go."

"The seats are up on the third tier but straight across from the stage. They should be great."

"Thanks, Scott. This is wonderful."

"Scott? You called me Scott," Wes said.

"Oh, I'm sorry, Wes. I'm really sorry."

"Annie, I know you don't know me very well, but I've got a feeling about you."

"What's that?" She grabbed the edge of her pillow, rubbing the material together. The edges of the lawyer's pillowcase were embroidered with little blue chickens.

Wes said, "I guess you think I'm too forward, but when I moved to Atlanta, I met so many people who were wrapped up in themselves, they couldn't bother to be considerate, so

I vowed I'd be friendly and helpful to others like myself who came here from out of town."

"I really appreciate that, Wes. You've been real nice to me."

"What are you and Scott doing today?"

"Oh, I have to look for an apartment." Andrew had told her to say she was looking for an apartment, so she would sound permanent.

"Well, let me know if I can help you out. And I'll give you those tickets Wednesday at work."

"Thanks, Wes. Talk to you later."

She threw a chicken-trimmed pillow at the wall, wishing she had invented a different excuse for settling in Atlanta— an institutionalized mother would have been good. Was there a Betty Ford branch on the East Coast?

At the animal shelter that afternoon, Annie chose the first dog she saw, a young shepherd mix. When the dog's gaze caught her eyes, he seemed to recognize her, and she didn't know how she could reject a dog she had communicated with that way. When she offered him her hand, he sniffed it shyly. His black-tipped ruff was sensuous and thick, like a heavy rug. Out on the street, pulling on the leash she had brought, he carried his tail in a way that made her think of Mick Jagger prancing across the stage.

"Come on, Mick," she said. "It's you and me now."

The dog jumped into her car without hesitation. His trust overwhelmed her. She remembered her father telling her about the Judas goat—a goat kept at a slaughterhouse to trick sheep into entering the killing room.

"I won't betray you," she said to the dog soothingly. She hadn't realized how much she had missed having a dog.

She thought Mick would be immense when he was fully

grown. He smelled bad. He sat on his haunches in the back seat, drooling on the cushion. When large trucks passed, he jerked his head around and snapped at the window. Annie drove around the edges of the city, counting the times she saw the word "Peach." She loved to drive. She realized she was talking excitedly to the dog about things the dog didn't understand. She actually said to him, "Atlanta is the home of *Gone with the Wind*." And "Beware of religions that have water slides"—a bumper sticker she saw.

He behaved better in the car than in the condo. He explored restlessly, then hid for two hours under the bed. He ripped up an ancient copy of *Time* with the ayatollah on the cover. He wolfed down anything she offered him—kibble, canned turkey, bits of fish from a frozen diet dinner. She gave him a chocolate-chip cookie, then remembered something she had read about chocolate being fatal to dogs. She wasn't sure. Outside, Mick explored the small yard, digging under a bush and anointing the azaleas. He barked at all the cars entering and leaving the parking lot. Sometimes he seemed to be meditating, sitting upright and motionless with his eyes closed.

At midnight Annie shared a couple of boiled eggs with Mick, and they watched Bette Davis in *The Great Lie*. Annie wished Wes would call back. She imagined telling him Scott had drowned. Or joined the Air Force. Tumbleweeds of dog hair had drifted up against the baseboards in the hall. She wondered if Clayton Scoville was allergic to dogs. She tried to imagine the lawyer. A handsome, unattached guy rolling recklessly down the Zambezi in a bright yellow raft with a rollicking group of people—all pink-cheeked and footloose, flirting their way through the tentside gourmet meals prepared for them each evening. He was probably a jerk, she thought.

During the night she heard Mick's toenails on the parquet of the foyer, then heard him scratching at the carpet, probably at the spot he had sniffed persistently since his arrival. His senses were so different from hers, his perceptions total mysteries to her. She could look at the dog and the moisture dotting the sponge of his nose like fresh rain and then feel a kind of pleasure she hadn't felt since high school. In the morning she called her father with the news about the dog. "Now you're cooking," he said.

At work on Wednesday, Annie paid Wes a hundred and fifty dollars for the Rolling Stones tickets, even though he protested that she didn't have to buy both of them. Actually, she intended to bill Andrew for Scott's ticket. It was only fair, she thought.

During the evening she observed Wes's calm efficiency while directing the waiters, checking on supplies, absently stroking the sticky ficus as he made friendly small talk with the clientele. She saw him standing by the dish station in deep conversation with Theresa, who always split for the bus stop as soon as she was off, anxious to get home to her kids. Theresa's teenage boy had to appear in juvenile court on a shoplifting charge, and Wes listened sympathetically. Sometimes Annie thought Wes was a slick operator, and sometimes she thought he was as innocently sincere as one of those religious fanatics waiting for the Rapture—except that in his case the Rapture was the Stones concert. Which made it O.K., she thought, her heart pounding.

As they were closing up later, she impulsively invited him over to meet her dog.

"What if Scott catches us at your place?"

"He won't," she said.

He followed her in his car. As she drove, she was aware of

his lights in the rearview mirror, as if they were spotlights exposing her life. He whistled in admiration when they entered the condo. "I didn't know you were rich, Annie. Boy oh boy, will you marry me?"

"I couldn't afford this place even if I get to switch to cocktailing," she said, laughing. "It's just temporary—a friend of a friend."

Mick was barking. When she let him in through the kitchen, he leaped on her joyously, his nose cool against her cheek and his tail thumping the wall. But when Wes entered the kitchen, Mick backed into a corner, cowering.

"He shouldn't do that," Wes said, with concern.

"He's kind of shy," Annie explained. "He hides under the bed a lot."

She gave Mick a scrap of steak she had brought from the restaurant, but she had to hold the molded-foam carry-out box of scraps high out of his reach. He leaped for it a couple of times. So she set it on top of the refrigerator. He circled the kitchen, his claws scraping the tile.

"He'll control you if you don't start training him," Wes warned. "Giving him that scrap just encouraged his bad behavior."

Annie bristled at Wes's schoolteacher tone. "Well, he likes me just fine," she said, wrapping her arms around the dog. Mick nuzzled her hand and she stroked him gently.

"He could turn out to be a fear-biter," said Wes.

"Do you want a Coke or something?" Annie said impatiently. "I don't have any beer and I don't drink anything hard."

Mick was still jumping on her, so she fed him a bowl of dry food along with the remaining steak scraps. While eating, he growled and eyed Wes. Annie put Mick outside when he had finished.

"Do you want a boiled egg?' she asked Wes.

"No, thanks. A Coke's fine." Wes was studying a bookshelf.

"I always have a Coke and a boiled egg after work. I don't know why. A habit, I guess." She decided not to eat an egg in front of him. She scattered a bag of tortilla chips into a bowl and set it on the coffee table.

"I saw all these books about sports and thought there might be something about dogs," Wes said.

"No. I already looked. The guy who owns this is real outdoorsy, but I don't think he's the type to tie himself down with a dog."

To get Wes off the subject, Annie played a Stones tape and asked him about his family. They sat in the living room on the vast leather boomerang couch. He rotated his Coke glass on its coaster as he talked. He said, "I'm the middle child of five and the first one in my family ever to go to college. My brother's at Auburn now. We weren't poor, but we had to budget. Daddy works for the state, and Mama works at the J. C. Penney's at the new mall in my hometown? They're better off now than they ever were, but they don't know how to take it easy." Wes settled comfortably into the leather and crunched a handful of chips. He continued, "Mama had a pretty hard time when she was growing up. She always said they were so poor they didn't pay attention." He smiled and dug into the bowl again. "I never knew what she meant, but I guess it was her way of saying they didn't have time for anything but work. When she sent me off to college, there was this look on her face, like I was going to move into another world and turn my back on her. So now, even though I work in a fancy restaurant, I call her and Daddy twice a week. I always send birthday cards and Mother's Day and Father's Day cards. I'll never forget that look on her face." He smiled. "It's funny what families go through, how involved it is."

His voice was like cotton, clean and absorbent. Annie was aware of her dog barking, of the late hour, of the bump of the bass on the song that was playing. Wes kept talking. She didn't know what to say when he paused, signaling her turn at a confidence. She felt her way along slowly, talking vaguely about childhood feelings, her ambitions, her take on Atlanta ("like one of those World's Fairs"). She admired the way a slight curl on his hairline didn't want to conform to his precise, expensive-looking haircut. She heard a car pull in next door, then the storm of barking.

"Excuse me, I'd better do something." Annie let Mick in carefully, holding his collar. Immediately, he hid behind the corner easy chair.

Wes stood up to go. "You know, Annie, they're saying at work that you're a spy from corporate," he said, facing her.

"I don't know what to say," she said, fumbling with the glasses and coasters. Heart in proverbial throat, she'd say to Andrew.

"I don't know if that's true, and I won't ask you, but generally speaking it's a pretty sad state of affairs when a company can't trust its own employees and has to send in outsiders to check up on them. It's like Russia."

"Not anymore," she reminded him. She went on, babbling. "I know what you mean. It's getting hard to know who to trust anymore. People everywhere saying they're sincere, and they *seem* sincere, but at the same time they're living a bold-faced lie."

"You mean a bald-faced lie."

"I thought it was bold-faced? Like a headline."

Wes was yawning. He rattled his car keys in the pocket of the blue windbreaker he was wearing. "I didn't mean to hurt your feelings," he said, turning the doorknob. "Anyway, I think you need to work with that dog a lot. It'll be a challenge."

"I do need to learn more about dogs," she said, yawning back at him. She wondered if yawning was contagious with dogs and decided to try it with Mick later.

After Wes had gone, Mick paced through the room, sniffing. He lifted his leg against the couch where Wes had been sitting.

"Bad dog!" Annie yelled. When she returned from the kitchen with some paper towels, she saw Mick with the lawyer's fur-lined cap, which had somehow gotten out of the closet. She lunged at the dog, crying, "Drop that, Mick! No, Mick!"

Mick ripped an earflap from the hat. When she tried to take it from him, he growled possessively. She retrieved the cap, but he kept the earflap.

She dropped to the floor and cradled the dog's head. "O.K., Mick," she said. "It's time for a heart-to-heart."

She located Andrew on his car phone.

"What do I do now? I think I blew it."

"Hold tight," said Andrew. "I may fly you out pretty soon."

"O.K. This is too confusing. I'm ready for a change."

"Good girl."

"What about my dog?"

"Why did you get a dog, anyway?"

"Because I wanted a dog."

"What kind of dog?"

"A German shepherd mix."

"Good dogs."

"Andrew?"

"Yeah."

"Don't say 'good girl.' It sounds like 'good dog.' "

"Right." He paused and she could hear a car horn on his line.

"I've got a car," she said. "Do I have to fly—with the dog?"

"You could drive. Fine. Annie? I'm sorry about this. It's not your fault. I think word got out somewhere else. But this is part of it, you see." His voice was exuberant, punctuated with traffic sounds. "You did your job. Now we know somebody's on the lookout. They're nervous. Something's going on."

"Well, I know I didn't let on. Maybe somebody saw me scribbling a poem on a napkin and thought I was taking notes on them."

"Why would you write a poem?"

"Same reason I wanted a dog."

"Funny. O.K., Annie. Get a good night's sleep. Contact me tomorrow night after work, and we'll decide what to do next. I'm thinking Birmingham. Either that or Little Rock."

Annie was thinking the Riviera. Or the Zambezi. She imagined hitting the road with Mick. The dog seemed to like riding in the car, and she saw the two of them adventuring together, a team—like the Lone Ranger and Tonto. Lewis and Clark. Harry and Sally? She couldn't remember many adventure duos, but she was sure there were plenty. She wondered if she should stay in this kind of work. Wes had thrown her. She had been trying to perform the job she was hired to do, and her parents, after all, had sent her to college so she could get a good-paying job. But they thought that majoring in hotel management meant she could start running a hotel the day after graduation.

When she let Mick outside later, he began barking immediately. She grabbed his collar and told him to stop, but he barked harder. She couldn't get him to yawn when she did, either. He whimpered, then pawed the ground in an embarrassed way. A car horn sounded, and he slammed against the fence, barks flying out of his throat like a water pipe bursting.

Before work the next day, Annie stopped at the public library to get some books on dog care and training. Wes was right about her dog. She had a nut case for a pet. She had left Mick in the yard, barking his head off. She didn't know how high he could leap, or what neighbor might poison him. By next week, she could be far from Atlanta. She would have to mail the books back.

She checked out half a dozen dog books—obedience, nutrition, canine history, even a guide to the sure-fire way monks train German shepherds. Later in the restroom, Annie noticed a woman standing next to a pallet she had made in the corner. She was listening to a small radio through earphones. Suddenly the woman thrust her hand into Annie's face. Annie saw the broken nails, polished bright orange. The hand was chapped. Annie flinched.

"Got any spare change?" the woman was saying.

Annie dug into her purse and found a handful of coins. The woman dropped the money into the side pocket of a tote bag bearing an art museum logo. She was perhaps in her forties, with uncombed shaggy hair and several layers of shirts and vests. Her aqua pants, splotched with brown stains, were stuffed down into shiny red rubber boots.

"Hey, you, get offa my cloud," the woman muttered in a thin singsong voice. "It's all you hear. The Rolling fucking Stones will make more money in one night than my mama made in a lifetime."

"You want a ticket?" Annie said impulsively. "I've got an extra ticket." She set down her books and plunged her hand into her purse, unzipping the compartment where she had stowed the tickets.

The woman laughed sarcastically. "Well, let's see. I don't

have anything on my social calendar, and I'm not going on a Caribbean cruise this year. I must have money to burn."

"No, I mean, I'll give it to you. I'm not a scalper. I'll just give it to you."

The woman studied the writing on the ticket, her mouth moving silently, her face expressionless.

"Just pretend you won a prize," Annie said, backing away and leaving the restroom. Instead of waiting for the elevator, she ran down the stairway two flights to the exit, pausing to show the library books to a guard. She was confused about what she had done. By the time she reached her car, it occurred to her that the woman might just sell the ticket and buy drugs. Annie tried to imagine who might show up in the seat next to hers. It was like anticipating a blind date. It was an interesting thought—one that stopped her for a moment in the act of pointing her key at the ignition. She realized an important fact she hadn't mentioned to Andrew. She couldn't leave Atlanta until she had seen the Stones. And she wouldn't. So what if he fired her.

At work Wes was painstakingly swabbing the ficus tree with cotton balls soaked in alcohol. "Every damn leaf," he said proudly. "I came in early to do this and I'm almost finished."

"The tree looks great," she said, amazed that anybody would go to such lengths. Wes seemed joyful as he stood back and surveyed the gleaming tree—the life he'd saved.

"You seem nervous," he said.

"Really? Oh, I guess I am. I guess I wasn't prepared for the big city, after all." She told him about the woman in the library. "I gave her my extra ticket. Scott's not going."

"Good for you," Wes said as he shifted the tree back into its accustomed spot. He collected the cotton balls and wadded them into the business section of the morning paper. He wiped his hands on a napkin.

"Do you want to go eat after work?" he asked. "I know this barbecue place. It's just a hole in the wall, but the barbecue is out of this world. They've got practically a whole cow on a big table. You pull the meat off with tongs and put it on a piece of refrigerator cardboard and they weigh it. It's your basic meat-and-slaw place, but it's better than this wimpy French stuff we serve here."

Annie stared at Wes. Enthusiasm was running out of him like the bubbly fountain outside, with its atmospheric lights that operated even in the daylight.

"It's my apology," he said. "I wasn't too nice last night."

"That's O.K."

"Let's go eat and I won't say a word about your dog—or your boyfriend."

"I got some dog books," she said. She gazed out the window at the traffic. "What in the world is refrigerator cardboard?"

Wes was giving some answer, an effusive description that she half heard, intending to store it and savor it later. People were getting off work, and the sidewalks were a blur of similarly dressed business people—shadowy, layered images interweaving like a flock of birds swirling together. Her eyes zeroed in on the only spot of brilliant color in the scene—a woman's yellow basketball shoes, the color rising and falling, boats chopping at the gray waves.

Three-Wheeler

Checking the dirt-streaked window, Mary saw the little boys slipping around through the woods again. They were sneaking from tree to tree, hiding. Today they had their rifles with them.

She let her pottery wheel die and stomped outside. The boys were brothers, and they lived two houses down the road. Their small white house appeared to be barricaded, with its hedge of oil drums and chicken crates.

"What are you boys up to now?" she said, rubbing her clayey hands with an old dish towel. They beamed at her with calculated innocence.

"Do you need us to kill you some snakes?" the older one, Jeb, said, fixing her with a sly Humphrey Bogart gaze. He was about ten.

"No. What do you want to kill my snakes for?"

"They might get in your clubhouse," the smaller one

said. His name was Abe. He was freckled like an old blue-enameled dishpan.

"You've got a neat clubhouse," Jeb said, tossing his head half an inch.

He was talking about her pottery studio, the little shed tacked on to a storage barn. She spent all her time there, throwing pots. She didn't have time for little boys or anything considered normal around here—cooking, TV, church. She was sure these boys had picked all her daffodils last week.

"Do you need us to kill you any groundhogs?" Jeb said.

"I haven't seen any groundhogs."

"It's a dollar-fifty for a groundhog, ten dollars for a snake," said the younger one.

Jeb shifted his rifle. He said, "Abe specializes in snakes. I'm after foxes, but ain't many of them. And the coyotes are whomping all the groundhogs."

"I don't need you little boys around here," Mary said, hiking her coveralls up.

"Don't you have *any*thing that needs killing?" Abe said.

"We can help you do stuff," said Jeb.

"I don't need your help," Mary said. She motioned toward the "clubhouse." "Don't let me catch you messing around *there*."

Pointing their rifles ahead, they disappeared around the corner of the barn, where there was a padlocked door. "What's in there?" Jeb asked when she reached the boys.

"That's where my ovens are," Mary said with a dangerous grin. "My ovens are so hot they would melt those guns of yours. Now don't let me catch you fooling around here or I'll shut you in my ovens."

"We ain't scared," said Jeb.

"Don't you know what happened to Hansel and Gretel?" she asked.

Their blank faces said no.

"That's pathetic," she said. "Don't your parents teach you anything?"

She was certain these boys had killed the birds she kept finding scattered throughout the woods. Earlier in the month, she had found a pile of songbirds beside a tree. The shattered birds looked as though they had gathered for a songfest and sung themselves to death.

The next day, from the kitchen window, she saw the boys sneaking out from behind the barn. Yanking along a small wagon, they ran through the woods. They skidded into the new mound of dirt she had had delivered and began digging. She had gotten the dirt to fill in a place where an old out-house site was sinking, but it had been dumped ten yards away from the hole. A latticework of roots covered the depression in the ground.

Again, she rushed out to face the boys. "What are you doing?" she barked. "Quit messing in my dirt." She paused to collect herself but then blurted out anyway, "I know what you boys did to my March flowers. You're thieves and vandals."

She pointed to the picked patch, a few yards away. She imagined the daffodils still nodding their heads, like a reflex action.

"We want to work," Jeb said. Their sincere faces were shining up at her like cut flowers. The younger one was pudgy, with sandy hair cut in a line across the middle of the back of his head, as though he'd had a run-in with a Bush Hog. He said, "We need to help out at home 'cause Mama's lost her job and has to get oddities."

"That ain't it, Abe. It's *com*-oddities," Jeb said slowly.

"Cheese and sacks of no-'count stuff," said Abe, making a face.

"What are you doing with my dirt?" Mary asked. Their wagon had some of the new dirt in it.

"We was going to help you move it—fill in that hole." Jeb was suddenly a funny sight, the way he was acting like an experienced building contractor.

Mary studied the little boys closely. It had been hard to get help since she inherited this unmanageable property from her uncle. She was busy with pots. She had orders to fill for the spring catalogs, and she was behind with her outdoor work. Leaves were falling when she moved in last October. She hadn't raked or mowed. She knew the frontage must be kept clear or she'd get fined, but the point held no urgency for her. The barn was full of machinery that she had not troubled herself to use. Recently Mrs. Hayes, a neighbor down the road, dropped by to chat and snoop. She said, "Your uncle always cleaned out the woods and picked up the limbs and kept it mowed like a park. But you've got all them flowerpots and sandbags. That's not how your uncle kept this place."

Mary, instantly spiteful, thought of the woman as the Nasty-Nice Neighbor, but she took out an ad in the paper for a yard man. One fellow said he would come and mow the woods, but he never came. Another took the job, raked leaves for two hours, and then went home with a headache. He called later to say he was allergic to leaf mold and had to quit. Then a woman called and accused her of running a sexist ad. Mary dropped the ad. Sometimes she just didn't think, she told herself. Most of the time she just didn't think. She had to focus on one thing at a time. She was here, not in Santa Fe. She had to make the pots, fill the orders. She had abandoned everything else, on the advice of Henry Thoreau, who said, "Simplify, simplify," and Henry Ford, who said, "Simplicate, then add lightness." Ford was speaking about his formula for airplanes, but it would apply to anything, she thought.

When she visited here as a little girl, the shed was her playhouse. She played in these woods, where these little boys now explored. The woods were thick then, shielding the outhouse from the road. One year when she came back to Kentucky to visit, Uncle Bob and Aunt Reba had a new bathroom with lime-green imitation tiles. That tileboard had now buckled from the mildew behind it.

"Well, maybe I could use your help," Mary said to the boys.

They wore loose, baggy jeans and had their baseball caps on backwards. Their little wagon was rusty, and in one end it had yellow scum and wads of clotted comic books.

"We can weed-eat," Jeb said to Mary.

"We weed-eated our fencerow yesterday," Abe said. "Mama said we done it good."

"Let's just fill in the hole," Mary told them. "It's where an old outhouse used to be. I want to fill it in where the tree roots are showing."

"We need us a dump truck," Abe said solemnly.

Maybe his hair had been trimmed with a weed-eater, Mary thought. "Do you know what an outhouse is?" she asked.

They shook their heads.

"I'll bet you've never seen one."

Their faces lacked all curiosity. She might have said, "Environmental Protection Agency" and aroused more excitement.

"All right," she said to the boys. "If you can move that dirt and fill in the hole this afternoon I'll pay you five dollars."

"Ten," said Jeb. "There's two of us. Five dollars apiece."

She grunted an O.K.

The boys got to work. She watched them from the clubhouse, where she was shaping a medium-sized pot. Her pottery was simple and functional, not like the useless multi-textured art pieces she used to make out in Santa Fe. She had

O.D.'d on artiness—all moonshine and selfishness, she decided. Her pieces were no better than the glitter-dusted ceramic frogs and elves Aunt Reba had collected. Now she supplied plain clay pots to a mail-order company that sold them as bread-loaf bakers, with recipes. She tried baking bread in one of them, but it seemed a silly and clumsy thing to do.

Every few minutes she glanced up, to check on the boys. What an odd pair they were, with old-men names. They even spoke like old men.

It was hard to concentrate on the spinning mud while the boys were there. She gave up and went outside. She began burning leaves in the trash barrel. Then the boys came up behind her, startling her.

"You can't burn till four-thirty," Jeb said. "When the wind dies down."

"Is this any of your business?" Mary asked, heaving leaves into the flames.

"They'll get you. They fly over in helicopters a-looking for people burning."

"And they look for Mary-Juanita," said the little one.

"How do you know that?"

"Daddy said."

"How much dirt have you boys moved? I'm not paying you for Sunday-school lessons."

"We need your riding mower to pull our wagon, so it'll be faster."

"That's silly."

"We can make twice as many loads."

The idea tempted her. She could get the mower out. She had filled it with gas before the yard man's two-hour visit. A two-hour yard man ought to be twice as good as a sixty-minute man, she thought, remembering the raunchy old song. She always thought it should be the theme song for *60*

Minutes. Her mind was flying around loose. She was suddenly eager to look at the equipment in the barn.

She went indoors for the key to the barn. Uncle Bob and Aunt Reba's decrepit old house resembled an antiques mall, with random collections of grimy old stuff. Mary had cleared out a couple of rooms for her needs and crammed the bric-a-brac into the other rooms. She shoved away the needlepoint pillows, the artificial flowers, the Coca-Cola memorabilia—Bob and Reba's lifetime.

The boys followed her to the barn. Abe was dragging a tobacco stick. With another stick, Jeb was whipping at bushes. "Leave those bushes alone," she said. "They'll bloom soon, and you're not going to pull their heads off when they do."

She opened the barn. Inside was a treasure trove of equipment—a leaf blower, several mowers, a riding lawn tractor, and a three-wheeled all-terrain vehicle.

"Wow," said Jeb. "A three-wheeler!"

"Gah," said Abe. His mouth hung open.

She sent them to work with the riding mower, but before long they were back again, bursting right through her clubhouse door. She was about to spin off a pot. She kept working with fierce concentration.

"You need to get that three-wheeler out and ride it some," said Jeb.

"No, I believe not." The pottery wheel slowed to a whisper.

"It'll rust out if you don't ride it."

Abe said, "I want to ride it."

"Have you got that dirt moved?" The pot gleamed, shiny and fresh.

"We need that three-wheeler," Jeb said. "It'll pull the wagon better."

"The tire's flat," she said.

"We've got a pump at home. We'll go get it!"

They took her vague nod for "yes" and went flying home.

She loaded some pots into a crate to carry to the kiln. She liked the way you could bake something into place. She liked the illusion of permanence in something so fragile as pottery.

In a few minutes she saw the boys coming through the woods with a pump. They had entered the barn and pumped up the tire of the three-wheeler by the time she reached them. Jeb had the gas cap off and was feeling inside the tank with his fingers.

"She's good to go!" he cried.

She thought how satisfying it would be to take a willow switch to these boys.

Jeb said excitedly, "Our papaw said he ain't seen none of these three-wheelers since heck was a pup."

"Papaw's at our house," Abe said. "He sleeps all day, but he woke up and got us the pump."

"I don't have a key to this thing," she said.

"It don't use a key. It has a button," said Jeb. He was already starting it up. "If we hook it up to the wagon, we can pull the dirt a lot faster."

"We're good workers," said Abe. "We're worky-holics."

They were already driving away, like a bus she wanted to catch, pulling away without seeing her signal. They were racing across the woods. Abe held on behind Jeb. The three-wheeler was buck-jumping. She ran along behind them to the pile of dirt.

"You've got too much dirt," Jeb said. "We need to take some down to the creek down there."

He pointed beyond the bushes to a small creek on her boundary. Even in April, it was only a trickle.

"If we had a bale of hay, we could load it on the wagon and we could ride it down there and make us a dam," Jeb said.

Mary shook her head. "If you dam that up, you'll flood the whole bottom."

Jeb said, "If we had some beavers to come, they could make a good dam."

"They could make it with sticks," said Abe. "And trees."

"We could catch some fish if we had a pond," Jeb said.

"We could catch some beavers, too, if there was a dam."

"Now don't you go damming that up," Mary said calmly, as if they were having a reasonable discussion. "There are no beavers here, and if you dam up the creek, Mr. Smith's pond over yonder will dry up and we'll have a pond here. That's like stealing somebody's pond."

She saw the gleam in the older boy's eyes jump like an electrical spark over a synapse to his brother's eyes. She said, "Now go on and finish spreading that dirt like I hired you to."

She went back to her work. She had to spin another set of pots. She cut the clay and slapped it angrily on the table. She didn't believe the boys would fall into the pit where the outhouse had been, because of the tree roots, but if they did it was their own fault. They were pestering her. She slapped the clay down. She pumped the wheel and helped the mud spin into shape. The little boys were moving dirt. They wanted to make a dam. Making a dam would be like making a clay pot. Had they really said the three-wheeler would rust out if it wasn't ridden? She shivered. She thought about the last time she had had sex. Her doctor said regular sex kept the tissues healthy.

The next time Mary glanced at the woods it was full of boys—at least a dozen of them, all sizes. A raggedy-haired one was driving the three-wheeler pell-mell through the bumpy woods. The boys whooped and squealed. The woods reverberated with their ruckus. The dead birds suddenly jolted her mind. She could imagine the pile of bluebirds and robins, their decomposing bodies clustered as if they had come together for a sacrifice. She felt remote from the scene, as if it were happening on TV.

She went inside the house to the bathroom. She was startled to see a vague hag in the mirror. She thought she should try a mud pack on her face. She had plenty of clay for it. There ought to be a glazing technique to preserve the face.

The telephone rang.

"I've seen what's going on in your woods," said the Nasty-Nice Neighbor. "I'm afraid those little boys are going to get hurt."

"I'm watching them," Mary said impatiently.

"Bob Burney used to let the boys around the neighborhood ride that three-wheeler, but then they passed a law against those things. Didn't you know that? What if one of them little boys gets hurt? Have you lost your mind?"

"Are you going to call the police?" Mary shot back. "Why don't you have us all arrested?"

"I don't want to fool with the police," the Nasty-Nice Neighbor said. "You can't trust them."

"How do you know I didn't give that three-wheeler to those boys?" Mary said. "If they own it, then what they do with it is their responsibility."

"Well, I was just calling to let you know somebody might get hurt and they'll sue you to kingdom come. I don't like to meddle, but I figured I'd call you instead of the police. That's not how we do things around here."

Mary slammed down the telephone. Her muddy handprint wrapped the receiver like a sleeve.

The three-wheeler was headed for the creek. A skinny, dark-haired boy was driving, and he was picking up speed. The machine bucked and snorted. The troop of boys was running behind, trying to catch him. They jumped the creek with him, splashing through the shallow water. The boys were all yelling and shrieking, clamoring for rides. She hadn't realized that three-wheelers were outlawed now. Where had she been? But why should she know such a thing anyway? She realized that if they were illegal, it was probably illegal to buy or sell them. She had counted on getting some money eventually from the yard equipment. She shivered at the cold possibility that if she were angry enough, she could let a kid get hurt.

The mud on her hands was caking dry, drawing her skin taut. The leaf fire was almost out. The smoke had turned in her direction. If she hollered, the boys wouldn't hear her—the wind was wrong. They weren't listening anyway. She was just a strange, unkempt woman, baying at the wind. In another setting she would be taken for a bag lady. The bag part would be easy. Aunt Reba had saved paper grocery bags, a thousand bundles of them.

"Let me show you how to drive this thing," she said when she reached the boys. They surrounded her—hard little bodies, steamy and dirty, all in droopy clothing. She said, "I know a few tricks. I can ride this thing like a broomstick. Remember that scene in *E.T.*? The bicycles in the sky? Do you realize what witches can do on a contraption like this?"

Jeb shoved the dark-haired boy off the seat and let Mary take it.

"That would be funny, to see you ride," said Jeb, with his Humphrey Bogart manner. "Come on, y'all. Let her ride." Let's see the dame give it a whirl.

"She might take off on it and we'd never see it again," one of the little boys said with a worried pout.

"Is she *really* a witch?" a boy with a burr-cut said to Jeb.

The burr-cut boy's T-shirt said,

SEVEN DAYS

WITHOUT PRAYER

MAKES ONE WEAK

"Witch isn't even the half of it," she said. She settled herself, grabbed the handles and tested them. Giving it gas, she aimed at a line of open-mouthed boys, little pups who jumped as she headed for them. She gunned the overgrown tricycle over the rough ground through the trees. She passed the stump where the bluebirds and robins lay heaped like Jonestown victims. Skirting the outhouse hole, she shifted into a higher gear, then higher. She drove the three-wheeler out into the road, picked up speed, and waved good-bye.

As she rode, she dreamed about David McAllister's Harley, how she had mounted it behind him and they thundered down a dark country road rimmed by low natural walls of red rock. It was the spring of 1983, in New Mexico. She hugged his hard stomach and smelled his back, her face on his seasoned leather. She recalled that night on the motorcycle as vividly as if she were seeing a movie in her head. There she was, riding snugly behind him, feeling unafraid and buoyant and blessed with youth. Earlier, she had heard the Harley growl to a halt outside her house, and he came in carrying a dozen hot tamales wrapped in newspaper. He waited while she dried her hair. He microwaved a cup of coffee left in the pot from that morning. She asked about his dog, who had run away. He was happy, because his dog had come back. She was happy because he was happy. The grease from the hot tamales smeared the kitchen table, where they sat for a long while, falling in love. And then they went for the night ride through the canyon, undulating with the road.

When she saw him for the last time, he was in a hospital in a cloud of cocaine. She said good-bye to him, but he didn't hear her. She drove west on Route 40. The hue and texture of that cloud around him seemed to be projected out onto the giant scrub-board sky. It was as though his mind were spewing waste against the blue vault. He always used the word "waste." He could have been an architect, she thought. He saw all landscapes as constructions—the vistas and lines of rocks and sand and scrub and sky. A wasteland, he kept saying. She couldn't keep loving someone who would squander the sky itself. That was the last time she let herself be in love. He was only one small event in her past, one of those unmanageable pieces of her life that she had swept under the road as if the road were a rug, and now here she was in Kentucky, looking for road signs. But she was still riding that Harley. She remembered seeing, in the bike's swooping light, an owl the size of a small child standing by the side of the road. It revolved its head and rose—with marvelous, slow grace—into the blank night.

The Funeral Side

On her first night home in two years, Sandra McCain slept in her mother's old sewing room. Her own room had been filled with furniture from the store downstairs. One side of the first floor was McCain's Furniture and the other side was McCain's Funeral Home. As a teenager, after her mother died, Sandra worked in the furniture store; and as children, she and her brother had played hide-and-seek between the parallels of the divans. Now, since her father's stroke, a small staff operated the furniture store, but the funeral side was closed.

During the night, she heard her father's cane stab the hallway floor. She heard the commode flush.

Earlier that evening, as they sat on the balcony watching lightning bugs, her father said, "Well, Sandy, so you decide to come home to your old daddy when you think I'm going to kick the bucket."

"I'm glad to see you still have the funeral-parlor manner," she told him. He always turned on the charm downstairs, but upstairs he was plainspoken. The stroke was mild, but it had weakened him. "We never used to have flowers like this out here," Sandra said. The balcony was framed by half a dozen swinging baskets of fuchsias and geraniums.

"Damn place has always been full of flowers."

"But these are so friendly, not like all those horrible glads and mums that were always downstairs."

He made a fist, then released his fingers, an exercise to work out the deadness in his arm. "When are you going to marry and settle down?"

"You always ask me that. You seem to forget I was married once."

"How come you didn't stay married?"

"We wanted different things."

"A man and a woman always want different things," he said.

"Well, Dad, I sure don't see how the human race has survived."

He grunted. "What's it like up there in Alaska anyway? Is it like that old show *Northern Exposure?*"

"Not really."

In Alaska, the long summer light was beginning, so the darkness down here in Kentucky felt unnatural. From the balcony, the moonless sky seemed claustrophobic, but the lightning bugs winked little glimmers of hope.

Her father had been in this dying town all his adult life, putting people to rest. Surely his work had distorted his perspective, she thought. In high school she had hated him—or hated his work anyway. But now she regretted the distance between them. Her impulsive marriage was years ago, when she was in her early twenties. She and Wayne were married at Herrington Lake, near Lexington. Her father had a funeral to direct and did not come. At the end of the ceremony, the whole wedding party dived off the limestone palisades, like penguins. When she saw the wedding photos, her mind superimposed tuxedos on the guests. Wayne was large and comfortable with himself. He had dozens of good qualities. One of them was his simple sincerity. Another was the way he thought well of people, regardless of their flaws. Wayne was in graduate school, studying engineering, and Sandra was getting an M.A. in communications. One night, in the middle of a chapter called "The Dysfunction of the Mass Communicated," she suddenly threw the book across the room. She never went back to class.

In the morning Sandra brought her father a cup of herb tea and a bowl of granola. He was sitting on the balcony in a recliner from the store. By now Sandra had readjusted her image of him to include the new gray in his hair, the larger bald spot, the paler cheeks.

"I don't want that stuff," he said, making a face at the cereal.

"It's good for you." She had already lectured him on cholesterol and fat. "This is what I eat in Alaska."

"We're not in Alaska," he said. "I read where people should eat what's right for their climate. That's why Eskimos eat whale blubber and the Chinese eat rice. Don't you eat blubber up there?"

"Why am I trying to talk sense to you?"

He grinned. "I read about this health-food nut who lived to be a hundred and had never eaten anything impure. He went on one of those fasts that are supposed to be so good for you and starved to death." As he laughed, his cane fell to the floor.

"I'm not sure what you're driving at," said Sandra, retrieving the cane.

"If I had denied myself for a hundred years, I'd be calling for a bottle of whiskey and a big box of Goo-Goo Clusters at the end." He laughed. "Would you bring me whiskey and Goo-Goo Clusters on my deathbed?"

"Anything you say, Daddy."

Sandra returned to the kitchen and swapped the granola for a carton of eggs. She wondered if he was just being stubborn about his diet, or if his line of work had taught him something about dying. He was too young to die. The thought of his death made her furious—partly at herself, for waiting so long to come home.

Sandra pedaled around town on her father's bicycle. Cork (Pop. 1,700) was surrounded by cornfields stretching across the flat bottomland. The hardware store had closed long ago, but the florist's shop, the tiny grocery, the post office, and a gas station still lined Main Street. McCain's, one of the half-dozen large old houses in town, was faded yellow, and its wood siding was warped.

She crossed the railroad tracks and rode out past the water tower and the Christmas-tree farm. They always had a tree for the store, another for the living room, and a third for the funeral home. Once, a child had died just before Christmas, and the family brought the child's presents and set them under the funeral tree. After the burial, Sandra's father returned the packages to the grieving parents, together with the guest register and the thank-you cards. The family kept the gifts, unopened, under a small silver tree in the girl's bedroom. Now Sandra realized that she might have only imagined the silver tree.

She rode for two miles or more, passing house trailers and occasional new brick ranch houses. After being in Alaska, she thought this landscape seemed small and tame. There was not much wild left, although the new houses appeared to have sprung up like funguses in the fields. Alaska was far away. She tried to imagine Tom Girardeau at the Riverside Restaurant late at night, while the sunlight lingered. She pictured him ordering beer and steamed clams and insect spray. They often sat there for hours, watching the floatplanes take off and land on the Chena. She was sorry to miss solstice. Tom would go with friends up to Eagle Summit, where the sun seemed to crawl horizontally across the sky.

On the way back into town, she stopped at her widowed aunt's house. A red pickup was parked on the street, and a boy was mowing the yard. Aunt Clemmie, Sandra's father's sister, had tried to mother her and her brother, Kent, after their mother died, but they resisted. Sandra had been fiercely secretive and would never confide in Clemmie—not about her nightmares, or her grief, or her condemnation of her father.

Clemmie let Sandra in the side door. "I bet you wish you had some of this weather up there in Alaska, Sandra. Don't you freeze your behind up there?"

"You get used to it." Sandra fingered a warm jar of strawberry preserves on the kitchen counter. Just then the lid popped as it sealed. "I love the snow," she said.

"It snowed here the second of March," Clemmie said. "It killed the peaches."

"How do you think Dad's doing, Aunt Clemmie?" Sandra asked as she absently patted the cat, a haughty Persian with a breathing problem.

"Oh, honey, I don't know. The doctors said the arteries in his neck are blocked and that wasn't a good sign. But since you came home, he's doing so well! I see color in his face I haven't seen in months. He's real proud you decided to come home."

"I don't know what I ought to do," Sandra said as they moved to the living room. She sat in an easy chair spotted with doilies.

Clemmie said, "That brother of yours hasn't been down since Claude was in the hospital. But he works so hard and has a family."

Her aunt's tone was apologetic—Kent could be excused because he had responsibilities; Sandra had no responsibilities, since she had gone to Alaska voluntarily and was not married to the man she lived with.

"It was just extraordinary your daddy did what he did," Clemmie said, inviting the cat into her lap. "Raising you and Kent by himself and operating those businesses." She laughed. "We used to tease him about people coming to view the body and then on the way out shopping for dinettes. 'Dine *now*, die later,' we'd say." The cat looked at Clemmie admiringly, as if she were telling him stories. Clemmie went on, "Claude had a time with you kids. Oh, you fought him and he couldn't do a thing with you. He blames himself for the way you turned out."

"How's that?" Sandra said sharply. The cat glared at her.

"Well, your divorce and the traipsing around you do. He worries about you up there. He's afraid you'll freeze or get eaten up by a bear."

"He never said that."

"Claude never let on about his personal feelings. But he forgives you."

"Forgives *me*?"

"Don't go blaming him for everything, Sandra," said Clemmie gently. "That's the way with everybody these days."

Sandra settled her head back against a crocheted doily and listened to her aunt chatter. She imagined herself a cadaver, her head resting on a satin pillow, with lace framing her face. If she stayed here in Cork, she would just keep sinking until she lost all feeling, like someone in a sensory deprivation tank.

When Clemmie had phoned about the stroke, she begged Sandra to come back home. She said, "He always claimed he didn't need anybody, but he's been lonesome since you kids left. You probably don't even remember what a fun-loving man he was before your mother died, you were so young, but losing her made him draw up in a knot."

Sandra did remember. She remembered the night her father erected a teepee on the balcony for her and Kent when they were little. It was fashioned from a faded funeral canopy. Her father made hoot-owl and ghost noises in the night to scare them while they camped in the tent. She remembered evenings when they churned ice cream on the balcony, and he teased her mother, pinching her playfully on the rear. Sandra's mother had her hair fixed every Friday morning at Maybell's Beauty Parlor, to be nice for the weekend. And Claude inevitably joked about her hairdo. "Did you sleep in your hair wrong, Sally? It looks lopsided. Have the squirrels been in your hair?" When she was dressed up and had her makeup on, with bright red lipstick, he would say, "Your mouth looks just like a hen's butt." Back then, the balcony was the center of their life. It seemed to suspend them up in space—away from the crowded furniture, away from the bodies in the dark parlor. It was as though they were riding in a hot-air balloon. They watched thunderstorms from the balcony.

Two years ago, when Sandra's plane circled low over Fairbanks, the first thing she noticed was the bright neon sign of a Safeway. Sandra had promised herself she would stay two years in Alaska, and she had. She stayed there longer than she was married, longer than any of her stretches of school or jobs. She wrote her father occasional postcards, reports of bears and moose, with pointed references to how cold and wild it was. She went to Alaska with only a duffel bag, the remnants of her belongings from ten years of moving around. The only loss she regretted in all her wanderings was the dog she adopted in Lexington after her divorce. She was working at the human-services agency and lived in a basement apartment in one of the refurbished old houses on Maxwell Street. Her pet had the energy and endurance of a sled dog, she thought later. He loved to stay outside in the winter, his coat thick and glossy, even when the water in his dish was frozen. He had been poisoned, the veterinarian told her after she found him dead. He was stretched out on his side, at the basement entrance, as though he had been trying to get indoors. There was a puddle of blood under his tail.

Tom Girardeau kept sled dogs, but Sandra never grew attached to them. She had expected sled dogs to be beautiful, but most of Tom's dogs were skinny mixed breeds, not huskies or malamutes. He said, "People will run anything that's fast. They run hounds, shepherds. I even heard of somebody running a Scottie. And there's a guy who's trying to cross huskies with coyotes." Tom's doghouses were inside an enclosure adjoining a shed, where Tom had hung old saxophones and trumpets on the siding. Sandra almost expected a spontaneous concert to occur, with the dogs howling in accompaniment. Once, when she and Tom were canoeing, they passed a group of sled dogs on the riverbank. The dogs were on top of their houses, howling in chorus. It was near midnight, in that mellow light of early summer.

Sandra lived with Tom in a log house near Fairbanks, on the south slope of a hill with a view of the Chena River. On clear days they could see the jagged ridge of the Alaska Range, mountains crinkled up like freeze-dried clouds. Tom worked for the state agency where she had found an office job. In the dead of winter they rose at three in the morning to warm up the car. When she moved in, he had said only half-mockingly, "I can already see the day you'll move out. How long will you last out here in the elements?"

"I might last longer than you think," she said stubbornly.

"No, I can tell. You're Southern. Your blood's too thin." He seemed a little sad.

He had been in Alaska long enough to know exactly at what temperature the car's engine would freeze, exactly how many layers of clothing to wear in what weather. He knew how to dry salmon, how to repair a canoe. He had built the outhouse and the sunspace, where he was able to grow a few salad greens. He had come to Alaska to work on the pipeline and stayed because he fell for the frontier lifestyle—if living by necessity could be called a style, a point they argued about. She thought he romanticized hardship as much as she valued change. The dog team wasn't necessary, and he kept more dogs than he needed for one sled. The dogs' energy was like a basketball team in action. In the night, Sandra found their howls comforting music. The darkness grew tight around her in the winter, as if it cut her off from the rest of the United States and stranded her there on a horn of land on the noggin of the continent. Sandra lost her sense of time in the first long, dark winter. Four A.M. and four P.M. seemed the same. But as she stayed on, she learned that there was no pure division between light and dark. It was always becoming lighter or darker, like the moon inching through its phases.

When Sandra learned about her father's stroke, Tom encouraged her to go take care of him, insisting so emphatically she felt he was pushing her away, as if he were asking her to go out with another man.

"If you don't go, you'll be sorry the rest of your life," he said. "You have to go work it out with him."

"What do you mean?"

"You blamed him for what he did to your mom."

"She had a kidney disease. She didn't catch it from him."

"That's not what I mean."

"He never told me how serious it was," she said. "He didn't let me visit her in the hospital. I didn't know she would die."

"So now you won't trust any man."

"Don't I trust you?"

"No, you don't," he said. "If you did, then you could say you love me. You never say you love me."

Late that winter, Tom set out early one morning, running the dogs on some trails toward Nenana. He did not return until after the sun had come and gone. She was worried, even though she knew Tom had clear rules about the cold. He carried sled-repair equipment, ice creepers, camping gear, even a sewing kit and extra plastic booties for the dogs. As the dark deepened and she shoved more wood in the stove, she thought she heard a dog yelp, but it was only the wind. At last, in the moonlight, she saw the dogs coming, their shadows cavorting on the snow. Tom, still exhilarated by the run, went about routinely warming dog food on the stove. His cheeks were flaming, and ice crystals matted his beard. Looking outside at the dogs, still frisking, she felt foolish. She wondered if her anxiety was only cabin fever, her desire to be on the trail to somewhere else. The next morning, fresh snow had obliterated the doghouses. The dogs used the snow for a blanket. They burrowed, breathing through little blow-holes.

When she left for Kentucky at the end of May, Tom drove her to the airport. On the way, they saw a ski team racing down the highway on short, wheeled skis. In town, when the summer light came, the children snaked through the streets on skateboards. Tom used a three-wheeler to run his dogs in the summer. Before Sandra boarded the plane, she told him,

"I don't know when I'll be back." She knew he thought she wouldn't be back at all. Yet she didn't know how long she could bear to stay at home.

In Alaska, she had seen a dog that looked amazingly like her old pet—the same facial markings and coloring, the same shy, agreeable expression. He was in a pen in a small settlement where most yards were littered with the tattered remains of frontier living—oil barrels, rusted refrigerators, snowmobile carcasses. The tiny post office was having a rummage sale on its porch. She thought of trying to buy him, but she decided it would be a great mistake to get a new dog so much like the original. It would be unfair.

On the balcony, as they sat together in the evenings, she tried to tell her father about her life in Alaska, nervously straining for words to describe the height of the mountains, the glaring brightness of the snow, the brilliant colors of the wildflowers, the size of the mosquitoes. She realized she was exaggerating everything. There seemed to be no realistic way of describing the mosquitoes—the size of dragonflies, she said, almost as big as those remote-controlled toy planes she had heard when she was biking past a field outside Cork. She had automatically looked up for a bush plane and had momentarily visualized herself sitting at the Riverside having a beer while floatplanes landed on the Chena and the mosquitoes buzzed like friendly visitors around her head. Now she realized she was exaggerating to her father partly because she couldn't remember; there wasn't a clear line drawn between the ordinary and the fantastic in her mind.

One night she tried to describe the northern lights to her father. The night was humid and sheet lightning flared in the distance. "The aurora is like neon signs, and it works on the same principle," she said. Words failed. She thought of the pulsating colors and showers of brilliant light, sometimes described as a Chinese dragon undulating through the sky. She said, "The Tlingit Indians say the lights are spirits of the dead dancing—happy spirits. Some others believe the spirits are playing kickball with a walrus skull."

"I wish I could have seen that," he said softly. "I never got to go many places, holding down two businesses."

It made Sandra angry that he talked as if his life were nearly over. She said, "You could still go to Alaska. You're not even old. You've just been around death for so long it's rubbed off on you." She waited for a motorcycle to pass. "You could come and see me," she said.

The next day, Sandra drove her father's car to the library at the county seat and looked for pictures of the northern lights. She found a travel book that had a couple of photographs. The northern lights were nothing like she had described to her father. Although the pictures were not splendid, she realized that the lights were even more spectacular than she remembered—the sheer vastness of the space they covered, the implied shimmer and pulsation, the depth of the colors. They were more phenomenal than she could comprehend. She thought that sometimes sights and sounds were so unreal—like the news of someone's death—they could not be remembered or believed. She had exaggerated the mosquitoes but understated the aurora. She recalled what she had said to Tom when they saw the lights together the first time. She said they were like an orgasm. Later, during an orgasm, the curtains of color rippled through her mind. When she told Tom this the next day, he said, "It's like looking up a word in the dictionary and it gives you another word you don't know, and when you look up that one, it refers you back to the first word."

She thought if she showed her father the pictures, he

would not believe them; he would not believe his daughter could have experienced anything so magnificent. "You had to be there," she would have to tell him.

As the days passed, her father grew stronger, and Sandra stayed on in Cork, uncertain what she wanted to do. She felt she was testing herself, revisiting old memories and fears—the creepiness of living above a funeral home. Now that its doors were closed, she could imagine all the ghosts of the dead trapped in there. In her sleep, they hammered and clawed and whistled from the cavern below her.

Clemmie came over every day, sometimes bringing videos from the grocery. She cooked for them—fried chicken and ham and strawberry cake. Sandra's father battled his way around, brandishing his cane like a sword and swearing at life. He seemed almost his old self.

"I don't know when I'll be back," Sandra wrote to Tom. "Give my love to Brubeck, Coltrane, Satchmo, Thelonius, Dizzy, Billie, Mulligan, Miles, Fats. You may not believe this, but I love you."

The day after she mailed her letter, she received one from Tom. He wrote news of the dogs, the weather, the moose that visited the stream in the backyard. He was working an extra construction job in the evenings during the summer light and barely had time to scrawl notes to her. He didn't have time to run the dogs now, and they were growing desperate—howling and breaking loose. He was thinking of giving them up. Sandra could feel the dogs escaping, racing away from her, running faster and faster.

Sandra and her father were eating lunch. She had been helping out in the furniture store and had come upstairs to make some tuna salad. Her father said, "When I'm gone, you and Kent can fight over the business."

"Where are you going?"

"I think I'll close down the home for good. We never have more than two funerals a month anyway, and nowadays they want something fancier, or else they want to be cremated." He speared a cherry tomato—as expertly as Tom speared a fish, Sandra thought. He went on, "I always tried to make it homey, so people wouldn't feel out of place. It wouldn't be hard to turn into apartments."

"Who would want to live in it?" Sandra said.

"If you move out all the equipment and get rid of some of those morbid old carvings and lamps, you could have a pretty big apartment house here."

To Sandra's surprise, her father sobbed—a short belch of emotion. Tentatively, she touched his shoulder. He straightened up and cleared his throat.

He said, "There's something I want you to have—that old furniture of your great-great-great-grandfather's."

"Those old chairs in the sewing room?"

"There's more in the basement. I'll get it out when I'm able. I want you to have it when you know where you're going." He pushed his plate forward.

"It used to be in the dining room when I was real little," she said. "I haven't thought of it in years."

"I stored it away when your mother got all Danish modern upstairs. Your great-great-great-grandfather made that furniture—Thomas McCain."

"The one who started the business?" Sandra had only vague notions about such a distant past.

Her father nodded. "Thomas McCain was a carpenter, and in the old days, carpenters spent a lot of their time making coffins. So he's the one who started both businesses."

"Where did he come from?" asked Sandra, suddenly curious.

"He came here from North Carolina in about 1850,"

her father said as he reached for his cane. "He buried four wives and four children. He made their caskets, and it was such pretty work people started coming to him for their caskets."

"People died young then," Sandra said with a shudder.

"Later on, people started wanting to be embalmed and laid out in public. His son John McCain put out his shingle in 1889—Cabinetmaker and Undertaker."

Sandra's father stopped to reflect, as if he could actually remember that far back. "Thomas McCain had fourteen children, and his first four wives died in childbirth. But he kept going—kept finding new young wives to tend to all those babies." Her father laughed. "I always think about Thomas McCain when I take care of the dead. He's always in the background, giving me advice."

Sandra started hanging around the furniture store. The place could use a few new ideas, she thought.

"God, Daddy, some of this furniture down here looks like furniture from hell!" she yelled at him from the sidewalk. He was on the balcony, reading an undertakers' journal. "Only Satanists would buy it."

He hadn't said any more about the furniture he wanted her to have. She let the topic slide, not knowing what she would do with a collection of ratty old pieces. She didn't want to be responsible for them. Sandra rearranged the furniture in the store, making new combinations of tables and lamps and couches. She replaced the tacky dinette set in the window with plush love-seats. As a child, she had played with her dolls amid the clumsy pieces of furniture, and now she was playing there again. That was what she had always done with her life, she thought—play. In Alaska, Tom's log house was like a playhouse. She spent her time playing Scrabble with Tom, working jigsaw puzzles, making salmon quiche, building fires. She missed Alaska. In her memory it was warm.

Clemmie was sitting with them on the balcony, smocking a pinafore for a grandbaby. It wasn't quite dark. Teenagers on their way to the softball game passed below, jostling one another and screeching casual obscenities. Children on bicycles raced up the street, and barefoot kids tiptoed across the grass in front of the funeral side.

"Tomorrow is the longest day of the year," Clemmie said.

"In Alaska the sun will shine all night long," Sandra said.

Her father swatted at a bug. Sandra was annoyed that he and Clemmie had shown so little curiosity about Alaska. She felt twelve years old.

"In Alaska there's always something going on," she said calmly. "Something incredible to see."

Clemmie said, "The longest day of the year always comes sooner than I expect it to. I'm never ready for it." She laughed. "It gets dark so late I don't get indoors in time to watch my television shows. But they're all reruns anyway."

The telephone rang, and Sandra dashed inside to answer.

"I need to make some arrangements," a woman said.

"I'm sorry, the funeral home is closed right now."

"Well, Claude told me when my husband passed on he would make the arrangements. He had cancer, and he went about an hour ago."

"I'm sorry," Sandra said. "But my father's been sick. And the place is closed."

"I know. Is Claude able to come to the phone? This is Mrs. Bud Johnson."

Sandra recognized the name. Bud Johnson had been an old friend of her father's. She relayed the message. "What should I tell her?"

"Oh, mercy," said Claude, struggling up from his chair. "Tell Daisy I'll have him brought over. I promised."

"Dad, you're not able to do this."

"Oh, I can do it. I've got plenty of help." He nodded at her and Clemmie.

He grabbed the telephone and spoke soothingly to Mrs. Johnson. When he hung up, he stomped around the kitchen, punching the air with his cane. "Clemmie, get John over here to get the hearse out. It may need gas and oil."

John was his assistant, an insurance man who had helped at the funeral home part-time for as long as Sandra could remember.

"Claude, are you sure you're up to this?" asked Clemmie.

"John and I can do it if you two can get the place ready," he said, eyeing Sandra.

That night, she and her aunt opened the funeral side and aired it out. They plugged in large window fans and blew the stale air out—the stagnant sweet smell of powder and dead flowers and incense. Sandra had avoided the funeral parlor for years, but the smells were familiar. She shuddered and her lungs tightened. Clemmie hauled the industrial vacuum cleaner from the utility room.

As she turned on a chandelier, Clemmie said, "Now, Sandra, this won't be hard. We'll just clean up a little, and then tomorrow we'll take care of the details so your daddy won't have much to do at all."

"Dad doesn't seem sad," Sandra said. She realized her hands were trembling.

"Sad?"

"Bud Johnson was his friend."

Clemmie smiled. "They used to play in the hayloft when they were kids. They'd swing out on a rope and fly into the hay. Those boys would do anything for one another. " She punched the switch, and the vacuum cleaner roared across the carpet of the front parlor.

Sandra remembered Bud Johnson playing softball with

her father—with the Kentucky Lakers, a local team. When her mother died, Bud was around all the time; he brought ice cream on the day of the funeral. Sandra remembered it was chocolate chip. Yet she couldn't recall her mother's voice.

The funeral home was a maze—a scattering of rooms, furnished over the years with pieces from the furniture store—dark velveteens and brocades, dim lamps with romantic scenes painted on the shades, Early American tables. The place looked dilapidated, but strangely home-like. Sandra remembered her mother lying in the parlor, her head resting on a blue satin pillow, with her hair looking nicer than it ever had, and her lips bright and glistening, almost alive. Her eyes were shadowed uncharacteristically, her face deeply rouged. Sandra had seen so many dead people by then, she barely gave them a thought, but when her own mother lay there, she felt a deep betrayal, as though her father had been preparing all those bodies in anticipation of displaying her mother there one day, in a hairdo too perfect to tease her about. She vowed she would never forgive him.

As Clemmie vacuumed, Sandra peeked into some of the closed rooms. She entered the one with the cold metal table that cranked up like an elevator. Once, she and Kent had played doctor/nurse on the table, until their father caught them. He was there now, cleaning out a sink.

"Bud had that prostate trouble for seven years, and it finally got him," Claude said as he squeezed out a sponge.

The hearse arrived then, and some men deposited the body of his friend in the refrigerated room—what the family used to refer to, crudely, as the meat locker. Claude had turned on the refrigeration and it was already getting cool.

Sandra didn't sleep. In the early-morning hours she heard a car drive up, then a tapping on a door downstairs. She heard her father talking to someone. She remembered many times when deliveries arrived in the night. She remembered the quiet hearses. She remembered her father up at all hours, working secretly in the closed rooms. She was forbidden to enter the back rooms when he worked, and he always warned her and Kent to stay away from the Dumpster behind the building. For years, she had nightmares about her mother's ice-cold, bleached body. Again and again, Sandra dreamed that her mother was still downstairs, wandering through the rooms, a prisoner. Now she was afraid to sleep.

During the morning, flowers began arriving, and Clemmie and Sandra kept busy dusting and arranging chairs and vases. Sandra was quiet. Sleeplessness had aftereffects that were like grief, she thought. Claude and John had finished the preparations on the body, and some men had moved the casket into the front parlor.

"What a handsome devil!" Clemmie said when Claude appeared in a dark suit. "Claude, with that cane, you look like somebody in vaudeville."

"I don't even need it anymore," said Claude with a smile. "It's just for show." His step was sure and his voice stronger. He disappeared into a back room.

A boy brought an arrangement from the florist down the street. More flowers—the inevitable gladiolas and mums—arrived from another town.

"I hate this," Sandra said to Clemmie.

Clemmie brushed a wisp of hair away from Sandra's forehead. "I know, honey," she said.

Sandra plunged ahead. "What always bothered me was the way people always came to the funeral home and acted like it was some party, a social occasion. They always laughed."

"Now, Sandra. People do what they have to do," Clemmie said. "They can't just go around with a long face."

"They say the wrong things. They gossip and tell jokes."

Sandra was agitated, her head spinning. She might blurt out anything.

When her mother lay dead in this parlor, Sandra saw her father in a corner talking with Bud Johnson. Her mother lay on display in a casket, and Claude stood smiling, trading fishing stories with Bud. Sandra told Clemmie about it now. "I remember exactly what they said. Bud said, 'I caught forty bass in that pond, and I didn't even know it had bass in it.' And Dad said, 'That was *all* of them, wasn't it?' And he laughed. They went on like that. I remember it!" She pulled distractedly at her hair. "Everything about funerals is inappropriate," she said.

"Now, honey," Clemmie said, wrapping her fat arms around Sandra. "What should people say, Sandy? What would you have them say?"

Clemmie enveloped her like a down sleeping bag. Sandra pulled away.

"I don't care what they say. It's how they do. How could he have done what he did? How could he—how could he work on her? How could anybody do anything like that to anybody?" Sandra might have been crying. She wasn't sure.

"Get that out of your head," Clemmie said sharply. "He didn't do anything to her body that wasn't love. Maybell Cox fixed her hair, and I did her clothes. He got Roy Hicks over here from Hopewell to do the work."

"He did?" Sandra held on to a door facing. "I didn't know that."

"We told you that, but I guess you forgot. Why, you know Claude wouldn't treat Sally that way. He *couldn't* have."

"I always thought he did."

Clemmie hugged her again and Sandra didn't struggle. Clemmie said, "Why, Sandra, we had no idea you were bothered about that." She paused, pushed back, and gazed into Sandra's face. Her hands clasped Sandra's shoulders firmly.

She said, "But you never know what might be bothering a child."

Sandra said, "I didn't know she was going to die. Dad didn't even take me to the hospital except twice."

"Well, nobody knew she was going to die," said Clemmie, wiping tears from Sandra's cheek. "Besides, you said it depressed you to go to the hospital and see all those sick people. You were just a child. And you were busy. You were in the twirling competition, and you didn't understand."

"Twirling?" Sandra said. "I was *twirling?*"

In the afternoon, when the friends of Bud Johnson gathered, Sandra went to a dark nook upstairs where she used to hide out. Back then she couldn't escape totally from the laughter; now she had a small radio and earphones. She curled up in a nest of musty old cushions and tried to read, listening to some kind of New Age music that sounded like a stuck record. The station, broadcast from the college, called itself "the difficult-listening station." She forced herself to concentrate on the meaningless sounds until her head vibrated with the yelps of excited sled dogs racing in the bright snow, and she fell asleep. Eventually, Clemmie found her there.

"I'm all right," Sandra said, stumbling into the light.

"O.K., honey, I just wanted to know where you were," Clemmie said. "I saved you some chicken and some squash casserole."

Sandra crept down the carpeted stairs into the funeral parlor. It was empty, except for the casket. The lid had been lowered. Sandra heard her father speaking on the telephone in his office. "Now, Daisy," he was saying. "I knew Bud as well as anybody, and he wouldn't have wanted to stay hooked up to those tubes."

When he came out, Sandra said, "Hi. I fell asleep upstairs."

He laughed. "I'm surprised you could sleep in all this racket. Damn phone's been ringing itself silly." His fist opened and closed. "Now what?" The telephone was ringing again. Clemmie, who had followed Sandra, rushed to answer it.

"Are you feeling O.K., Dad?" asked Sandra as she straightened a wall carving of a youthful Jesus. It was made of plaster, with glitter scattered on it.

"That's one of those things I'm going to get rid of," he said. "Damn stupid crap." He grinned and stepped toward her. "I'm not leaving it for you to inherit."

"I don't want it," said Sandra.

"I don't want you to have it," he said. Leaning on his cane, he reached his free arm around her and squeezed her tightly. He whispered accusingly in her ear, "You ran off from home and didn't think about us."

"I came back, didn't I?" she mumbled, letting him hold her, more tightly than Tom had ever held her. She started to cry. She knew she could never explain herself to him, but that didn't seem so important now. It seemed more important to be kind. She said, "Dad, why don't you show me that old furniture you wanted me to have?"

He grinned. "How will you get it back to Alaska?"

"I don't know. FedEx?"

"Some of Bud's people are coming down from Akron, Ohio," Clemmie said, hanging up the telephone.

The next morning, the mail brought a letter from Tom. He wrote, "A bunch of us took a drive up to Murphy's Dome the other night, up beyond that old D.E.W. system with that white phallic tower. The wildflowers are all out. The lupines are as blue as your eyes. When I was up there, I thought about the time you and I were there and the wind came up and we almost got hypothermia. We were rushing around naked, and I realized I was sorry I'd accused you of having Southern blood."

She didn't get to finish Tom's letter—her father appeared, ready to show her the furniture in the basement. He had been too tired yesterday. As she followed him down the hall, Daisy Johnson and a swarm of kin arrived at the door.

Daisy said, "Claude's looking so well, Sandra. I didn't know it was you on the phone the other night. I never expected to find you at home."

"Did you think I would never come back?"

Daisy smiled. "Sandra, if you had a husband, you could take over this business from your daddy and let him rest some."

Sandra stiffened but held her tongue.

"I imagine I'll be closing the funeral home for good after this, Daisy," Claude said. "A little place like this isn't fancy enough to suit most folks nowadays. And some of them want to be cremated."

Daisy nodded knowingly. "Bud's sister-in-law in Florida is bad off and said she wanted to be burned and dumped in the ocean. I told Bud I wouldn't go all that way to Florida for the funeral if they didn't have the body."

"That's the trouble, Daisy," Claude said. "People don't want to do things right anymore. I was telling Sandy about her great-great-great-granddaddy. There was a man who did things right—because he was a carpenter. And if you're a good carpenter you're liable to do things right, don't you imagine?"

"Dad's threatening to give me some old furniture handed down through three or four generations," Sandra explained.

Claude said to Sandra, "I'm going to show you that furniture right now. Come on, Daisy. You'll appreciate this."

"Where is it?" Daisy asked. She was a small woman who didn't look strong.

"In the basement."

"Are you sure you can get down the stairs, Dad?" Sandra asked.

"Positive." He twirled his cane playfully.

"I'll stay up here if you don't mind, Claude," said Daisy. "It would be disrespectful to Bud."

"Well, if you think so," Claude said.

"Here, hold on to my arm," Sandra said to her father.

"You've done him a lot of good, Sandra," Daisy said. "I know he's missed you."

Sandra guided her father down the stairs, his cane clattering. Funerals bring out the best in him, she thought—and she was immediately ashamed. In her mind was a swarm of scavenger birds hovering around a wolf kill in Alaska.

In the basement, Claude turned on lights. He asked Sandra to move aside some boxes and picture frames. The furniture was arranged in a corner, set out as if it were a furnished room. A dining table with ladder-back chairs, a sideboard, a china cabinet, a washstand, a rocking chair, a hope chest. Sandra had half expected to see a child's coffin, but there wasn't one. The modern simplicity of the furniture surprised her. It resembled something in a Sundance catalog. It was beautiful. Her father must have gone to some trouble to arrange it here for her benefit. And now she saw he had restored it. The finish was smooth, and the wood was oiled and fresh, not dusty. The pieces were set out carefully, and so lovingly refurbished.

"When did you do this, Dad?"

"Oh, off and on for a few years. I needed something to do. Your mother always wanted me to fix it up." He started toward the stairs, then turned toward her. "I never got over your mother," he said. "When she died, it was like I disappeared for years. I thought nobody could see me."

Sandra was startled. She didn't know what to say, but she

let him hold her again. Then he turned away. She lingered in the basement while he made his way up the stairs. Daisy was beckoning him. Sandra studied the furniture, trying to imagine why her father, late in life, took up Thomas McCain's calling, as if his ancestor were in fact calling him. Was there a time in life when one's forebears suddenly insisted on being acknowledged? She imagined her father and Thomas McCain having strange conversations. Shop talk, she thought. The pieces were lovely, worn through time and use.

She could see her father at the top of the stairs, chatting with Daisy. Daisy had on an improbable pink pantsuit. She was smiling. Maybe they were laughing over old times, something funny Bud had said. Sandra could imagine Daisy and Claude becoming lovers. She remembered what her father had said about Thomas McCain and all his wives, how he quickly replaced the wives lost in childbirth. She pictured old Thomas jumping straight from the burial service into the urgency of courtship. But her father hadn't done that when her mother died. He was loyal to her memory. Sandra herself hadn't felt the need to honor tradition and continuity. She had gone off on a tangent from her history. Life seemed to her so strange, suddenly—the way people carried on, out of necessity, and with startling zest, at the worst of times. It was the stamina required by a bold adventure, a trek into the snow.

She heard a car crunching gravel in the lot behind the building.

Her father said, "Come on up here, Sandy. People are coming in, and the viewing's about to start. I need you to help me lift the lid."

Window Lights

I don't like the way the world is going nowadays, so I'm taking a break. A man gets tired of always striding out to gather trophies. A lot of guys who feel the same are just staying home with their guns. I'll stay here with my meager entertainments, waiting until the air clears.

I used to go on business trips, with my garment bag and briefcase hugging me like a little entourage. The last time I flew, the plane sat on the runway forever. On the P.A., the pilot apologized for the delay, saying we had missed our takeoff window due to inadequate federal funding for air-traffic control. I stared at the window by my seat. I noticed some strands of what appeared to be dog hair in the window. They were stranded between the two sealed ovals of plastic. The pilot announced that we would have to wait thirteen minutes for the next takeoff window. In my mind, I could see my little girl, gauging when to enter a jump rope turning before her.

Here at home these days, when I look out the window I can tell if the slightest change has occurred—a bird on the fence, a sprinkling of leaves on the neighbor's fish pool, a fallen branch from the sycamore tree. I notice any new colors and patterns of light. My grandmother called window-panes "window lights." And that was appropriate, since in her time windows were the main source of light. Grandma never turned on the electric bulb in her kitchen until it was far too dark to see and she had to feel her way around.

I recall her last years alone. I'd see her on periodic visits to Tennessee, where she had gone to live in the place she was raised. It had been a log house originally, in the pioneer style, with a shed roof above a porch and a breezeway called a dogtrot running through the middle. There was a chimney on each end of the house. My uncle Lon and his wife had lived there a long time. Lon was Grandma's oldest son. Lon and Bessie bricked over the logs and closed in the dogtrot. They added a wing and a lot of other things Grandma didn't like. When she moved back, she shut off the new part with the parlor and the picture window. Lon and Bessie bought a brick mansion with white columns in Nashville after he made it big in religious publishing. One night, Lon got drunk and smashed his car into a van of high-school wrestlers. He wasn't injured, but when he saw all those hurt kids scattered across the median he returned to his car and shot himself to death.

Grandma hated the picture window. "It don't set well with me," she said. It wasn't that she was afraid of people looking in, although by then a development had sneaked up around the house. She didn't like looking out at other people's houses and cars. She stayed in the back room, a nest she had made for herself with a path worn in the flowered-print rug. When I went to see her, I noticed her little nook had its own unique smell. It was a rancid smell of pork grease and old shoes and coffee and stale cornbread and age. She tuned in the local news on the radio every morning to learn the deaths, the weather, and the wrecks. But when Lon gave her a police radio one Christmas, she wouldn't use it. "It ain't right somehow," she said. "You're supposed to hear it on the regular radio, not like Eavesdropper Pop." She wouldn't use the telephone either. Lon and Bessie insisted she have one, for emergencies. Once, she lay on the floor for two days with a broken hip. She could have dragged herself over to the telephone, but she wouldn't. "Why, that hip commenced to heal, me a-laying there that way," she told me later in the hospital.

I sometimes imagine I am turning into my grandmother. Lately I've realized I am living on little but air and water and a few cans from the no-frills store. I've got drugs all the way out of my system. I don't drink anymore. I don't even take medicine. I'm laying low, observing, retreating, going off for forty days and forty nights, descending into the cave, maybe into the dark night of the soul—those clichés of mythic descent. I'm open to them all. My guide is the light of the television screen. Late at night, I have my pen ready to write down the toll-free numbers of the special offers.

It's peaceful. The cats politely ask to go outside. They bring back the news—a mouse, some feathers. In one way or another, the world comes to me.

And here comes Maddie, out of the blue. She called the other day. She moved back here to Lexington a month ago. I hadn't seen her yet, although she promised we'd talk when she got settled. She told me about her alienated-wives' support group, her skills-rejuvenation program, her trainee probation period at Luggage Land. I still love Maddie, and when she called and hinted that she wanted to end our separation, I was confused. I thought I did, too—she and Lisa are all I ever wanted—but I didn't think it should be easy for her.

She asked me if I was taking care of myself, eating right.

"I'm living on a dollar a day," I told her. That wasn't exactly true.

"How possible?" she demanded. "What can you get for a dollar?"

"You can get a can of hominy for forty-seven cents and if you mix that with a can of kraut you've got a pretty decent meal."

"Bill, are you trying to starve yourself?"

"Oh, another day I might eat oats," I said. "Not that instant stuff—you're just paying for packaging and processing."

"You can't live on oats."

"Why not?"

"You're just too lazy to cook. You're refusing to deal with food because I'm not there to cook for you."

"It's sociology," I said solemnly. "I'm running an experiment."

"Oh, come on."

"I'm an isolated, uncontaminated specimen. I'm studying the effects of TV on the blank and hungry slate of the human mind."

"You're making this up."

"Every day I write down an Insight of the Day," I went on, reaching for my journal. I shifted the telephone to the other ear. "Today I wrote, 'If you stay alone without speech, until you can hear yourself think, the universe will be opened to you.' "

"Have you tried counseling? I know a good—"

"I get plenty of counseling from TV. I just let things happen. I just wait at home till somebody on the tube tells me what I have to do. Isn't that what everybody does? Turn on the TV and somebody says buy this, eat that, don't eat that, watch this? What's so strange? Do you find that strange?"

"I guess I'm not really surprised." I could hear Maddie sigh, a last-straw kind of sigh. There's no kidding around with her. She always takes me so seriously. I thought she'd see I was trying to make light of my isolation—the fact that she tries to keep Lisa from me. But I guess there's a lot we've never understood about each other.

"You've got a frugal habit of mind," she said. "You always save food. You take the cracker packets home. And you save the jam jars and the soap from hotels."

"Maddie, I'm thinking a lot lately about people who don't have much to eat."

"But you can afford to eat, can't you? Are you trying to make a point about child support?"

"No. I'm thinking about people who don't have money to eat. The other day I chipped a tooth. I decided not to get it fixed. It makes me aware of all the people who can't get their teeth worked on."

"That's dumb. You'll lose your tooth."

"But people have always lost teeth. People used to be toothless by forty—if they lived that long. My grandmother didn't have a tooth in her head."

"I'm taking care of my teeth because they told me I'd have trouble with false teeth on account of this bone in the roof of my mouth? They said they'd have to cut it out to fit false teeth in. How'd you chip your tooth?"

"Popcorn." My tongue raked over the chipped place. It made a satisfying rasping feeling on my tongue, like sandpaper. I said to Maddie, "I can clean my tongue with the sharp edge of the tooth. You know how cats' tongues have those spines all over them?"

"I hope you're not going to get scurvy," Maddie said. "You at least need to take antioxidants." I could visualize her long black wavy hair, the little round knobs of her cheekbones. Those knobs were a motif all over her. Her beautiful shoulders and breasts reiterated her cheeks. I loved her knobbiness. Even her knees were appropriately shaped and beautiful.

"I want to kiss your knees," I said.

"I think you must be lonely," Maddie said. "And I can help if you let me."

"Help? What on earth can you mean? You can help by bringing Lisa back home. How is she? How are her teeth?"

"Lisa's fine. Her teeth are perfect. She's practicing her clarinet all the time."

"She won't play it for me when she comes over."

"You get on her nerves. She can't concentrate with you hovering over her."

What could I say to that? At least I wasn't drinking anymore. That should count.

It intrigues me that I don't get this tooth fixed. I never minded dentists. I always liked the laughing gas. It would send me on an adventure in the woods. The wallpaper at the dentist's is a mural of a forest landscape. Once, while getting a tooth filled, I was Hansel, leading my sister Gretel bravely into the forest. We met Little Red Riding Hood, asking for directions. She was going to her grandmother's. I accidentally sent her to the witch's gingerbread house. The child was really Lisa, in her Halloween costume. I see the significance of all that now, but I didn't then. Not that I have much confidence in the dream state. It's just stuff floating around, relaxing, stuff you mostly forget when you wake up because your memory receptors are shut off in sleep. That makes sense to me. The mind's swirling impressions and memories and capacities just let loose in a free-for-all. It's Dada. I think

Dada was thumbing its nose at Freud. Freud was a Victorian, and everything had to make sense to those people. Then the Surrealists and the Dadaists came along and turned dream symbols on their head and laughed themselves silly.

Just when my dreams start to make sense, there's a punch line, like Maddie calling.

Today, the morning newspaper tells about a homeless couple with two children. The husband is a Yankee, but the wife is sixth-generation Kentuckian, Scots-Irish to the bone. The husband lives under a bridge with some other guys, beside an open fire where they drink beer. He used to work with horses, but then he couldn't get work. She sleeps at the shelter with her two children in a single bed. She walks her nine-year-old boy to school. The school gave the boy a coat and some jeans and shirts and sweaters. He got to pick them out himself at the mall. He makes A's and likes to draw. The mother walks around town with the four-year-old girl till it's time to line up at the community center for a hot lunch. In the afternoon, they get the boy from school and play in the park until it's time to go find some supper. She says she doesn't like to keep her kids in those centers, around all those drunks, so she keeps walking.

I can get lost in a story in the paper and it starts to seem real, as if it's happening before my eyes. But of course it *is* real. I wish I could marry this unfortunate woman and take care of those children.

When Maddie came over to see me, I showed her the story.

"In New York they'd be living over a grate," said Maddie, dropping the paper on my broken wicker hassock. "They've got it pretty good here."

She looked around disdainfully at my place—what used to be our place. I admit I've let it go. She was on her way to work, and she had brought some doughnuts and coffee. She looked older, a bit hard in the eyes. Her cheeks were hollowed out. Her hair was cut short, and it flipped away from her face like wings.

"Come over tonight and eat supper with me," I said. "I've got a can of kidney beans and a can of corn."

"No, thanks. I can't tonight. Besides, I'd rather go out. What I'd like is some really good fettuccine Alfredo."

"Beans and corn are the prince and princess of nutrition. Millions of Mexicans count on them."

"I'm not Mexican."

"You're not Italian either."

"I bet your cats eat better than you do," she said, eyeing my lounging gray twins, Zippy and Bub. "You don't make them follow your diet, do you?"

"Oh, no, I let them have what they're used to. They're naturally thrifty anyway. Cats don't take more from the world than is necessary."

Maddie laughed so hard she roared. "Bill, you are still so naïve! What about all the songbirds cats kill? They don't have to hunt for a living, so they kill birds just for fun. They know they can depend on you for turkey-and-giblets or fancy-snapper-dinner, or whatever."

Whether she was right or not, I wouldn't agree. "They don't kill for fun. It's practice. Toning, keeping in shape. That songbird thing is erroneous. A neighborhood cat kills one cardinal and everybody blames the whole tragic loss of the world's songbirds on one cat. It's unfair." I attacked one of the doughnuts she had brought. It was delicious. "Are cardinals songbirds?" I asked.

She touched my arm gently. "Bill, I'm too busy for this role playing, or whatever you're doing. Did I tell you about my roommate's divorce? How her skunk of a husband testified that he had multiple personalities? He claimed he was faithful but that one of his personalities named Zeke was the one who went out with all these women. Can you believe such a story? He said he had five personalities, but she told me she could name six or eight herself."

On this topic I had nothing to say. That Lisa had Maddie's roommate for a sort of parent bothered me. I said, "Open your mouth. I want to see that bone you were talking about."

"No. Don't be ridiculous."

"I was trying to be romantic."

"Not now, please."

"I don't remember that bone in your mouth."

"It's just my brains pressing down. I've had a lot on my mind."

She turned to go, and I found her coat. "It was nice to see you, Bill," she said. "I don't really know what I expected."

As Maddie went out the door, I said, "I still love you," but evidently she didn't hear me. I remember the last time she let Lisa come here on a visit. Lisa was studying her geography workbook, her gnawed pencil flicking. I said, "You are the most wonderful child. I love you so much."

"That's good to know," she said, not looking up from her map of South America.

That night I heated my beans and corn in the microwave. As I ate, I watched *Wheel of Fortune*, then *Entertainment Tonight*. I ate slowly, concentrating on each bite. On *ET*, they discussed whether Elvis had been murdered, had committed suicide, or had faked his death. I think Elvis was in deep retreat, like me, and made a fatal miscalculation. They said Elvis put aluminum foil on his windows to keep daylight out, and he stayed up all night.

I don't know why Maddie and I were being so difficult. I have the feeling she wants to come back to me but is too proud to admit it. It is what I've wanted, but we don't seem to be able to make it happen. And, worse, I am losing our daughter. I also have the feeling that nothing is chosen, everything is inevitable—these fateful patterns of human behavior.

I sit in my easy chair in front of the television and write in my journal. My Insight of the Day: To avoid the trap of history, you've got to knowingly reenact it, go with it right up to the edge, then pull back. Then you're free. I have no idea how serious I am.

Surely what Maddie and I are going through is as old as time. If I could go back to the way we started out and try it again, I imagine following the same steps. When Lisa was born, Maddie triumphantly held the baby to her breast and said, "You see, Bill, here we are—indivisible." She saw something mystical in that union of flesh. But now it seems as if we had deposited ourselves in the fresh innocence of our baby, and we were left emptied out, disconnected. Eventually when Maddie left me, it was so sudden, without warning, it was as though she had yanked out my heart by the roots. I thought of those battlefield scenes where wounded soldiers hold their own innards in their hands like a newborn baby. When she left, she explained that we had to live apart in order to work out our differences. She was full of vague dissatisfaction. It was typical of the times, she assured me, making light of my despair. She had an offer of a job in Louisville—an opportunity to grow, she claimed. And Lisa could go to the ballet school there.

The weekends were confusing. Maddie made excuses to stay in Louisville. It took a while for me to realize the separation was bolstered by excuses and rationalizations—all contrived to accommodate Bradley Simpson, C.P.A. He was her goal all along. When I saw the separation was a devious scheme to admit him and his piggy eyes and his furry shoulders into her bed, I turned inside out like a sleeve. I was standing outside my own life, looking in. That's when I took to the bottle. Bradley Simpson is history now. It still makes me cross-eyed to think of him, but he is not important to our future, the story of Maddie and me. He didn't last, but our estrangement did. She liked her new freedom, her apartness from me. The inexplicable thing is now that she is back in town, I seem to be pushing her away. That is a flaw in me, like the desire to drink. Once things are set upside down, I don't know how you get them right again. I have to be forgiving, no matter the cost. If she is coming closer, I need to be receptive. But I haven't learned how. I have an instinct for the wrong move.

After supper, when it is dark, I get out my quilt pieces. What I'm up to isn't really a secret, although no one knows about it. And now I realize I want to surprise Maddie when it's finished.

Grandma pieced quilts at night, when she sat down to rest but needed to keep busy doing something practical. How she would laugh to see her grandson piecing a quilt! I'm sure she never knew a man who could even thread a needle.

I like to think I'm communing with Grandma as I sit here by the fire, watching television of an evening. She made wedding-ring quilts for the marriages of all her children. She quilted and watched *Bonanza* and *The Waltons* and *Little House on the Prairie,* all those frontier melodramas. I remember most fondly her sense of design, her love of color, and her overriding practical need to find a use for every scrap. She had the hots for Pernell Roberts of *Bonanza.* He wore a hairpiece and she wanted to rip it off in a steamy fit of passion. Or so I believe.

It's true that I didn't volunteer to Maddie—or to anyone—that I'm quilting. I know the significance they'd find in it. But somehow quilting makes me feel closer to Maddie and Lisa. Not that either of them would ever want to do such a thing. I also want to know what it's like to be a man improbably piecing a quilt. It's interesting: the clumsiness of my fingers on the needle, the times I've pricked my finger, the snip-snap of scissors through cotton. I lay the blocks on the floor and play with them for hours. Maybe I want to know what it means to be the kind of man a woman walks out on.

I'm not making a modern quilt, one of those ugly things made to hang on a wall. I hate those landfill collages— chewing-gum wrappers, plastic bags, tinfoil, bottle caps, all shouting a statement. I went to the Fabric Barn and bought yard-long remnants of delicate prints. They sell them especially for people making old-fashioned quilts because no one wears those prints anymore or keeps scrap bags. I know Grandma's scrap bags still exist somewhere in the old house. I need to go find them.

My pattern is a design I saw in a magazine. It is windows— many, many prisms all shimmering and reflecting the complexities of light. As soon as I pieced the first block, I could imagine the rest radiating from it, reflecting and interlocking and overlapping, like the light on a flowing river. It's all shades of blue—translucent and silvery and sky and dusk. Slate and rock and ice.

Grandma pieced in blues. I gaze into these windows and work toward the time when I get the quilt all pieced and can spread it out in the light. What I like best is the way the act of piecing the blocks is part imagination and part patience. It throws me outside time. It slows me down so much I feel like a Russian standing in line for hours to buy toilet paper. It becomes a meditation, stitch after stitch after stitch.

I won't tell Maddie about the quilt. I'll just wait and show it to her when I'm finished. I'll surprise her, and then we'll go back to the way we were. The quilt will be for our daughter, a present for her marriage someday.

Proper Gypsies

In London, I kept wondering about everything. I wondered what it meant to be civilized. Over there, I was so self-conscious about being an American—a wayward overseas cousin, crude and immature. I wondered if tea built character, and if "Waterloo" used to be slang for "water closet" and then got shortened to "loo." Did Princess Di shop on sunny Goodge Street? And why did it take high-heeled sneakers so long to become a fashion—decades after "Good Golly Miss Molly"? I wondered why there was so much music in London. The bands listed in *Time Out* made it seem there was a new wave, an explosion of revolutionary energy blasting from the forbidding dance clubs of Soho. The names were clever and demanding: the New Fast Automatic Daffodils, the Okey Dokey Stompers, Tea for the Wicked, Bedbugs, Gear Junkies, Frank the Cat, Velcro Fly, Paddy Goes to Holyhead. But the dismal, disheveled teens who passed me on Oxford Street made me think there could be no real music, only squall-pop, coming out of the desperation of the bottom classes. Yet I wondered what rough beast now was slouching toward its birth. I had an open mind.

However, I wasn't prepared for what happened in London. I was cut loose—on holiday, as they said in Britain. I had little money and no job to go home to, so this was more of a fling than a vacation. I had abruptly left the guy I was involved with, and now he was on a retreat (on retreat?) at a Trappist monastery. He had immersed himself in Thomas Merton books. Andy was very serious-minded and had high cholesterol. Actually, I believe he found Merton glamorous, but I always remembered the electric fan in India that electrocuted him—an object lesson for transcendental meditators, I thought. I was separated from Jack, my husband. New Age Andy had been my midlife course correction, but now he was off to count beads and hoe beans, or whatever the monks do there at Gethsemani. When he was a child, my son saw the dark-robed monks out hoeing in a field, and he called the place a monk farm. I didn't know what I'd do about Andy. He was virtuous, but he made me restless. I knew I was always trying to fit in and rebel simultaneously. My husband called that the Marie Antoinette paradox.

I was all alone in London, so in a way I was on a retreat, too. I had a borrowed flat in Bloomsbury for a month. My old college friend Louise worked in London as a government translator, but she was away, translating for a consulate in Italy. Back in the sixties, the summer after our junior year, Louise and I had gone to Europe together—"Europe on $5 a Day." During that miserable trip, Louise's mother died back in Jacksonville, and she was already buried by the time the news reached us in Rome. We didn't know what to do but grimly continue our travels. We ended up in England, and we took a train to the Lake District, where we met some cute guys from Barrow-on-Furness who had never seen an American before.

Louise's flat was on a brick-paved mews just off Blooms-bury Avenue. It stood at the street level, and all the flats had window boxes of late-fall blooms. There was no backyard garden—just as well, since I didn't want to mother plants. I wasn't sure what I wanted to do. I was supposed to be thinking. Or maybe not thinking. I wondered if I should go back to Jack. I didn't want to rush back automatically, like a boomerang—or a New Fast Automatic Daffodil.

Two days after my arrival from JFK, I still had my days and nights mixed up. On Sunday, I slept till well past two. After breakfast I went walking, a long way. I walked up Tottenham Court Road, past all the tacky electronics stores, to Regent's Park. I walked through the park to the zoo. When I got there, the zoo was closing. I decided not to proceed farther into the dim interior of the park but walked back the way I had come, on the wide avenue. The last of the sun threw the bare trees into silhouette.

As I walked toward the flat, I kept thinking about Louise. I hadn't seen her in five years, and we were never really close. She was always following some new career or set of people. She thrived on people and ideas, as if she hoped that any minute someone might come along with a totally new plan that would radically change her life. Her closet was a dull rainbow of business suits, with accessories like scarves and belts and necklaces looped on the hangers and a row of shoes below. Big earrings were stashed in the jacket pockets. There was nothing else in the flat that seemed personal, no knick-knacks or collections. She was without hobbies. No stacks of magazines, only some recent issues of *Vogue* and a lone *Time Out*. There was nothing to be recycled or postponed. The cupboards had only a few packages of Bovril and tea, and the refrigerator had been thoroughly cleaned out for my arrival. A maid was due each Thursday. I knew no one back home who hired someone to clean. In my neighborhood, in a small town on the edge of the Appalachian Mountains, if you hired somebody to clean or cook or mow, people would figure you had a lot of money and hit you for a loan, or they would gossip.

Louise's place was like a lawyer's reception room. The art on the walls was functional—a few posters from the National Gallery and a nondescript seascape. But in the hallway between the living room and the bedroom was a row of eight-by-ten glossy color photographs of plucked dead turkeys. The photos were framed with thin red metal edges. In the first one the turkey was sitting upright and headless, its legs dangling, in a child's red rocking chair. In the second, the turkey was sitting in the child's compartment of a supermarket cart. I could make out the word "Loblaw's" on the cart, so I knew the photographs were American. In the third, the turkey was lying on a rug by a fireplace, like a pet. In the last, it was buckled into a car seat.

I longed to show Jack these pictures. He was a photographer, and I knew he would hate them. The pictures were hideous, but funny, too, because the turkeys seemed so humanized. I had a son in college, but Louise had no children and had never married. Was this her creepy vision of children?

It was almost dark when I reached the flat. A sprinkle of rain had showered the nodding mums in the window box. Clumsily, I unlocked the outer door with an oversized skeleton key and switched on the light in the vestibule. Beyond was a door with a different, more modern key. I opened the second door; then a chill flashed through me. Something was wrong. I could see my duffel bag on the floor. I was sure I had left it in a hall closet. The room was dark except for the vestibule light. Frightened, I darted back out, pulling both doors shut. I jammed the skeleton key into the lock and turned it. At the corner, I looked back, trying to remember if I had left the bedroom curtains parted slightly. Was someone peeking out?

I walked swiftly to the nearest phone box, a few blocks away, and called the number Louise had left me, a friend of hers in case I needed help. It was an 081 number—too far away to be much use, I thought. A machine answered. At the beep I paused, then hung up.

I might have been mistaken, I thought. I could be brave and investigate. I walked back—three long blocks of closed bookshops and sandwich bars. It would be embarrassing to call the police and then remember I had left the bag on the floor. I had experienced deceptions of memory before and had a theory about them. I tried hard to think. Louise had assured me, "England is not like the States, Nancy. It's safe here. We don't have all those guns."

I had some trouble getting the outer door unlocked. I was turning the key the wrong way. I had to try it several times. When I got inside, I fit the other key to the second door, but it pushed open before I could turn the key. It should have locked automatically when I closed it before, but now it was open. I could see my bag there, but I thought it might have traveled six inches forward. Now I realized that the outer door may have been unlocked, too. My courage failed me again. Turning, I fumbled once more with the awkward skeleton key. Then I rushed past the bookstores and the sandwich bars to the call box, where I learned the police was 999, not 911.

"I think my flat has been broken into," I said as calmly as I could.

A friendly female voice took down the information. "Please tell me the address."

I gave it to her. "I'm American. I'm visiting. It's a friend's flat."

"Right." The voice paused. The way the English said "Right" was as if they were saying, "Of course. I knew that." You can't surprise them.

"I thought London was supposed to be safe," I said. "I never expected this." In my nervousness, I was babbling. Instantly, I realized I had probably insulted the London police for not doing their job.

"Don't worry, madam. I'll send someone straight-away." She repeated the address and told me to stand on the corner of Bloomsbury Avenue.

I waited on the corner, my hands in the pockets of my rain parka. People were moving about casually. The scene seemed normal enough, and I was aware that I didn't believe anything truly calamitous could happen to me. This felt like an out-of-body experience, except that I needed to pee. Soon four policemen rode up in a ridiculous little car. I had heard they didn't go by the name "bobbies" anymore. (Not P.C.? I had no idea.) Two of them stayed with the car, and two approached me, asking me questions. They took my keys.

"Stay here, please, madam, while we check out the situation." The bobby appeared to be about twenty. He was cute, with a dimple. His red hair made me think of Jack when we first met.

They whipped out their billy sticks and braced themselves at the door. It was a charming scene, I thought, as they entered the flat. I didn't want to think about what the cops in America would do. In a few minutes, the older of the two bobbies appeared and motioned me inside.

"Right," he said. "This is a burglary."

Inside, the place was like a jumble sale. All the drawers had been jerked from their havens and spilled out. The kitchen cupboards were closed, but the bedroom was a tornado scene. My clothes were strewn about, and Louise's pre-accessorized suits lay heaped on the floor, the earrings and necklaces scattered. I was so stunned that I must have seemed strangely calm. The police might have thought I had staged the whole affair. Louise's place had been so spare that now with things flung around, it seemed almost homey.

"Was there a telly?" said the bobby with the red hair.

It dawned on me that the telly trolley was vacant.

"Why, yes," I said, pointing to the trolley. "And there was a radio in the kitchen."

"No more," he said. "Was there a CD player or such?"

I shook my head no. Louise never listened to music. How could she like languages and not music?

"The TV, the radio, and about a hundred dollars cash—American dollars," I told the policeman after I had searched awhile. The cash had been in a zippered compartment of my airline carry-on bag. I had no idea what hidden valuables of Louise's might have been taken. My traveler's checks were still in the Guatemalan ditty bag I had hidden in a sweater. The burglars must have been in a rush. I had probably interrupted them. The phone-fax was still on the desk. The turkey pictures were hanging askew.

The bobbies wrote up a report. They gave me advice. "Get a locksmith right away and have the lock changed," Bobby the Elder urged.

Bobby the Younger beckoned me into the vestibule. "You see how they got in? The outside door should have been double-locked. See the brass plate of the letter box? They could poke an instrument through the slot and release the door handle inside. Then it was a simple matter to force the lock on the second door. It could be done with a credit card."

"It could have been Gypsies," Bobby the Elder said. "There's Gypsies about quite near here."

"Be sure to double-lock the outer door," the Younger reminded me when they left a bit later. He seemed worried about me. I tried to smile. I coveted his helmet.

Consulting the telephone book, I chose a locksmith named Smith because the name seemed fitting. His ad said, "Pick Smith for your locks." While I was waiting, I tried to clean up the place. I hid Louise's kitchen knives behind the pots and pans. I looked for clues. Under a book on the floor, I found a framed photograph of Louise's parents. They stared up at me as if I had caught them being naughty.

Smith came promptly, arriving with a tool kit and a huge sandwich—a filled bap, like a hamburger bun stuffed with potted meat. He set it on the dining table.

"You'll be needing a few bolts," he announced, after examining the doors.

"Could I ask you to block up the letter slot somehow?" I asked. I explained how the door could be opened through the slot.

Smith flipped the brass plate a couple of times. He frowned. "How would you get the post?"

"I'm not expecting any letters." Andy might write, but that didn't matter. Jack didn't even know where I was.

"I could screw it down," Smith said begrudgingly. He was a heavyset man who looked as though he worked out at a gym. He wore clean, creased green twill. Between bites of his bap, he shot an electric screwdriver into the lock plate of the living-room door and removed some screws. The sound was insect-shrill.

"Likely this was committed by some Pakis," he said, pausing in his attack. "The Pakis are worse than the Indians."

"I wouldn't know," I murmured. I was trying to remember where Lousie's parents belonged. I had tried them out in the bedroom, but they looked too disapproving.

"We have some very aggressive blacks," Smith went on. "Some of them look you right in the eye."

"I wouldn't jump to conclusions," I said. I plumped a sofa cushion.

"But you know how it is with the blacks in your country." A screw dropped to the floor.

I didn't know what to say. I wasn't used to hearing people talk like this, but as an American I didn't seem to have a right to object. "Have you ever been to America?" I asked.

"No. But I long to take the kids to Disney World." He scooped up the screw. "Maybe one day," he added wistfully.

After that, I toured London by fury. I walked everywhere, replaying what had happened, hardly seeing the sights. I walked right past Big Ben and didn't notice until I heard it strike behind me. "Eng-a-land swings, like a pendulum do, bobbies on bicycles two by two"—that song kept going through my head. I walked the streets, dread growing inside me. I saw signs on walls of unoccupied stores: FLY STICKERS WILL BE KNACKERED! It sounded so violent, like "liquidated" or "exterminated."

I found that I was talking to myself on the street. A teapot was a grenade. A briefcase could be a car bomb. There *were* guns. I remembered the time Jack and I went with our little boy to see the crown jewels. It was 1975, at the Tower of London. We were waiting in a long line—Louise would say queue—to see the royal baubles, and an alarm went off. A group of baby-faced young men in military uniforms materialized, their M-16s trained on the tourists. Any one of us might be an IRA terrorist.

The cacophony on the major streets was earsplitting. On

the Pall Mall, the traffic was hurtling pell-mell. The boxy cabs maneuvered like bumper cars, their back wheels holding tight while the front wheels spun in an arc. A blue cab duded up with ads screeched to a halt right in front of me and let me trot the crosswalk. Still angry, I marched to Westminster Abbey, aiming for the Poets' Corner. I had a bone to pick with the poets. Where were these guys when you needed them? I had to elbow through a crowd of tourists earnestly working on brass-rubbings. A sign warned that pickpockets operated in the area. I never followed directions and now I refused to ask where the Poets' Corner was. I was sure I'd find them, lurking in their guarded grotto. I walked through a maze of corridors, stepping on the gravestone lids of the dead. A great idea, I thought, walking over the dead. I stomped on their stones, hoping to disturb them. Then I saw an arrow pointing toward the Poets' Corner. But a velvet rope and a man in a big red costume blocked my way.

"Why can't I see the poets?" I demanded

"Because it's past four o'clock," the man in the big red costume said.

I didn't know the poets shut up shop at teatime. Slugabeds and layabouts. Pick a poet's pocket—pocketful of rye? Would prisoners have more self-esteem if their bars had a velvet veneer? I wended my way past a woman in a battery-powered chair that resembled a motor scooter. I skirted the suggested-donation box and plowed around a crash of schoolchildren.

I left the poets to their tea.

At the Virgin Megastore on Oxford Street, I searched for music. Everything was there, rows and racks of CDs and singles of folk and gospel and classical and ragga and reggae and rock and pop and world. The new Rolling Stones blared out over the P.A. No moss on Mick! Then a group I couldn't identify caught me up in an old-style rock-and-roll rhythm. I had to find out what it was. It was a clue to the new music, all the music I had been reading about but couldn't hear in the soundless turkey decor of Louise's flat.

"What group is playing?" I asked a nose-ringed clerk.

"Bob Geldof and the Boomtown Rats, from their greatest-hits CD," he said, smiling so that his nose ring wiggled. "Circa 'seventy-eight."

Where had I been all these years? Why didn't I know this? Did this mean I was old? The song ended. The Virgin Megastore was so huge and so stimulating I felt my blood sugar dropping. There was too much to take in. Whole walls of Elvis.

At the British Museum, I stared at ancient manuscripts. I saw something called a chronological scourge. It was a hand-written manuscript in the form of a "flagellation," an instrument used in ritual self-discipline for religious purposes. The chronicle was a history of the world, written on strips of paper streaming from the end of a stick. There was a large cluster of the shreds, exactly like a pompon. I wondered if Andy was flagellating himself at the monastery. A paper scourge wouldn't hurt. It would only tickle and annoy, like gnats. Birch bark twigs would give pleasure. Rattan would smart and dig. Barbed wire would maim.

For two days, I kept telephoning Louise, getting no answer at the villa in Italy where she was supposed to be. Then I got an answering machine, Louise in Italian. I guessed at the message, heard the beep, and blurted out the story. "Don't worry," I said. "There wasn't any damage. Just the telly and the radio and nothing broken. I had to change the locks." I asked her to let me know about the insurance. I didn't tell her about the gagged letter slot and how I found her mail littering the mews because I kept missing the postman. I knew she would say "telly" and not "TV." Louise had gotten so English she would probably have tea during an air raid.

I sat in a cheap Italian trattoria and drank a bottle of sparkle-water. The waitress brought some vegetable antipasto. Then she brought bread. I ate slowly, trying to get my bearings. I knew what Andy would do: purify, simplify, and retreat. He'd listen to his Enya records, those hollow whispers. I felt a deep hole inside. The family at a table nearby was having a jovial evening, although I could not make out most of their conversation. A young man, perhaps in his thirties, had apparently met his parents for dinner. The father ordered Scrumpy Jack and the son ordered a bottle of red wine. The mother pulled a package from a bag. It was gift-wrapped in sturdy, plain paper. The young man opened it—underwear!—and discreetly repackaged it. He seemed grateful.

Another young man arrived, carrying a briefcase. The two young men kissed on the lips. Then the new arrival kissed the mother and shook hands with the father. He sat down at the end of the table—diagonally across from the birthday boy— and removed a package from his briefcase. It traveled across the table. Some kind of book, I thought. No, it was a leather case filled with what looked like apothecary jars. The birthday boy seemed elated. He lit a cigarette just as a young woman swept in, wearing a long purple knit tank dress with a white undershirt and white high-heeled basketball shoes. Her hair was short, as if Sinead O'Connor hadn't shaved in a week or two. She handed the boy of the hour a present. I decided she was his sister. But maybe they weren't even a family, I thought. Maybe I was just jumping to conclusions, the way the locksmith did.

My main course arrived. Something with aubergines and courgettes. I couldn't remember what courgettes were and couldn't identify them in the dish. I didn't know why the Italian menu used French words. I wondered if Louise had learned Italian because Italy was where she learned of her mother's death. Maybe she had wanted to translate her memories of those foreign sounds we heard that unforgettable day at the American Express office, near the Spanish Steps, when she got the news from America.

Finally, I spoke to Louise on the telephone. "Don't worry about this little episode, Nancy," she assured me. She had no hidden valuables that might be missing. We discussed the insurance details. I'd get my hundred dollars, she'd get her telly.

"The police said it might be Gypsies that live nearby," I offered.

"Oh, but those are proper Gypsies," she said. "They don't live in the council estates."

Council estates meant something like public housing. "Proper Gypsies?" I said, but she was already into a story about how a cultural attaché's estranged wife showed up in Rome. The Gypsies must live in regular flats like Louise's, I thought. In America, no one would ever use a phrase like "proper Gypsies." Yes, they would, I realized. It was like saying "a good nigger."

"Louise," I said firmly. "I'm very disturbed. Listen." I wanted to ask her about the Indians and Pakistanis, but I couldn't phrase it. Instead, I said, "Remember when we went to Europe on five dollars a day?"

"More like six," she said with a quick little ha-ha.

"You know how I didn't know what to say to you when your mother died? I was useless, not a comfort at all."

"Why are you upset about that now?"

"I just wanted to tell you I'm really sorry."

"Look, Nancy," Louise said, in mingled kindness and exasperation. "I know you're unnerved about being burgled. But you got the locks changed, so you'll be O.K. This is not like you. I believe you're just not adjusted to your separation from Jack."

"It's not that," I said quickly. "It's the world. And the meaning of justice. Major stuff."

"Oh, *please.*"

"*Ciao,* Louise."

At a little shop I bought detergent and a packet of "flap-jacks," just to find out what the Brits meant by the term. I went to a laundrette: how did Louise do her wash? The laundrette had a few plastic chairs baking in a sunny window. Two Indian women cleverly bandaged in filmy cotton were washing piles of similar cotton wrappings. They were laughing. One said, "She was doing this thing that thing." She had beautiful hands, which she used like a musical accompaniment to her speech. It dawned on me that Louise's maid did her wash, probably taking it to her own neighborhood laundrette. I wondered if the proper Gypsies had maids. Technically, wouldn't a proper Gypsy be one that fit all the images? Gold tooth, earrings, the works? I sat on one of the hot plastic chairs. In my pocket I had a fax from Andy—a fax from a monastery! I didn't think I would answer his simple-Simon missive. I couldn't imagine a monk faxing. I waited in the laundrette, eating the "flapjacks." They were a kind of Scottish oat cake mortared with treacle. The Scottish called crumpets "pancakes." They had tea very late, giving the impression they couldn't afford dinner. But the English had afternoon tea just early enough to make it seem they didn't have to work during the day. The English said "starters" for appetizers, preferring a crude word to a French word. Their language was proper yet at times strangely without euphemism. They ate things they called toad-in-the-hole, bubble-and-squeak, spotted dick, dead baby. They ate jacket potatoes and drank hand-pulled beers. I couldn't decide whether this was terribly strange or very familiar.

I threw my jeans and T-shirts and socks into a spin dryer called The Extractor. It was a huge barrel encrusted with ancient grime and thick cables of electricity. It looked like a relic of a brutal technology. Dark satanic mills.

At Trafalgar Square, trying to get from Nelson's Column to Charing Cross, I got caught up in a demo of some kind. With my plastic bag of laundry, I squeezed among a bunch of punks with electric-blue and orange Mohawks. Spiritless teenagers in ragged, sloppy outfits propelled me through a flock of pigeons. I kept one hand on my belly-bag; the pickpockets from Westminster Abbey were probably here. Maybe poets, too. I couldn't tell what the protest was, something about an employment bill. I saw turbans and saris, and I heard hot, rapid Cockney and the lilt of Caribbean speech and the startled accents of tourists. I could hardly move. My plastic bag of laundry followed me like a hump. Although it was scary, there was something thrilling about being carried along by the crowd. I felt all of us swirling together to a hard, new rhythm. My hair was blowing. I could feel a tickle of English rain. A man next to me said "Four, four, four" and the woman with him beat time in the air with her fists. Her earrings jangled and glinted. The scene blurred and then grew intensely clear by gradations. It was like the Magic Eye, in which a senseless picture turns into a 3-D scene when you diverge your eyes in an unfocused stare. As you relax into a deeper vision, the Magic Eye takes you inside the pictures and you can move around in it and then a hidden image floats forward. Inside the phantasmagoria of the crowd, everything became clear: the stripes and plaids and royal blue and pink, the dreadlocks and Union Jacks. I saw

T-shirts with large, red tie-dyed hearts, silver jewelry, gauzy skirts, a large hat with a feather, a yellow T-shirt that said STAFF. I saw a coat with many colors of packaged condoms glued all over it. The surprise image that jumped into the foreground was myself, transcendent. All my life I had had the sense that any special, intense experience—a sunset, the gorgeousness of flowers, a bird soaring—was incomplete and insufficient, because I was always so aware it would end that I would look at my watch and wait. This was like that, in reverse. I knew the crush of the crowd had to cease. It was like an illusion of safety, this myth of one's own invincibility.

Finally, I reached a crosswalk where a policeman had halted traffic and was rushing people across the street. I landed in front of the National Gallery. I joined a smaller throng inside and found myself staring at some sixteenth-century Italian crowd scenes and round Madonnas. The thumping piano of "Lady Madonna" surged through my head.

I thought about the first time I visited England. It was in the summer of 1966, and I was alone in London for a few days because Louise had gone on ahead to deal with her mother's effects. It had been five weeks since her mother died. I was left alone, emptied of Louise and her grief. I was going home soon. The Beatles were going to America, too, to begin what turned out to be their last tour there. Their records were being burned in the States because John Lennon had commented offhandedly that the Beatles were more popular than Jesus. I figured he was right. The morning newspaper gave their flight number and departure time. It was a summons to their fans to wish them well on a dangerous, heroic journey. The Beatles' vibrant rebellion had taken a somber turn. I decided to go to the airport and try to get a glimpse of them because I was young and alone and I loved them fiercely, more than I'd ever loved Jesus. I took the tube to the Heathrow station, then had to catch a shuttle bus. While I was waiting, a motorcade turned a corner right in front of me. It was a couple of police vehicles, with one of those black cabs sandwiched between them. I realized it was the Beatles being escorted to their flight. I could see vague shapes in the back of the cab. I waved frantically. Through the dim glass I couldn't tell which was which. But I believed they saw me, and I knew they were thinking about America, cringing with dread at the grilling they faced. They were looking at me, I was sure, and I was looking at my own reflection in the dark glass.

The rest is history.

Night Flight

After she moved back to her hometown in Kentucky, Wendy was careful not to get involved with a good old boy, or any guy with a single redneck tendency, or any who watched TV sports obsessively. Then she met Bob Jackson. He didn't watch much TV. But he fished.

On a Friday afternoon in June, Wendy drove to Bob's weekend house in a small lakeside development with a marina. She wasn't sure where the turnoff was, but then she recognized the sign, LITTLE BLUE HERON ESTATES, with a clumsily painted bird—royal blue. Several new building sites had been gashed out of the scrubby woods, and a dozen or so modest houses lined the gravel road, which branched along the inlet. A sign in the yard of an A-frame said DUN-WORKIN. Nearby stood a bend-over—a painted plywood cutout of a fat woman bent over, her pantaloons showing beneath a polka-dotted dress. Bob's house, a chalet-style prefab, sat near the airstrip being constructed to attract weekend residents from all over the five-state area.

She found Bob at the marina, tying up his motorboat. When she kissed him, he tasted salty, as if he had been out on the ocean, not the lake. Corn chips, she realized.

"They're not biting," he said. "It's too calm. They get restful."

"It must be the drought."

He nodded and jerked his head toward the lake. "The crappie have gone out in the middle, in the deep drop-offs. Usually in early summer they hang around the banks."

Bob had sun-bleached blond hair with a reddish cast to it and a matching freckled complexion. His muscles were tan and hard. He was wearing a cinnamon tank-top and cutoff jeans, the raveled fringe hanging down unevenly and brushing his legs as he worked to secure the boat against the dock. He stuck his rod-and-reel and tackle in her hatchback, and they started down the short gravel stretch in her car. The minnow bucket sloshed at his feet. When her hand on the gear shift brushed his leg, he responded by caressing her bare leg up past the hem of her shorts. She pulled into his driveway, and he shot out of the car.

"Last one in the sack is a rotten egg!" he cried.

She had moved back to Kentucky from Florida only recently, and she was still tentative about returning to the place she had once been so eager to escape. But she had missed living in a place where life was slower and safer—the kind of place meant for raising families. In Florida, she had lived midway between the city and the beach. The motorcycle gangs arrived in February, followed by spring-break revelers. On her way to work every day, she drove past tomato fields. After the tomato plants began to turn yellow and the red fruit deco-

rated the fields, the pickers arrived. One day they were suddenly there, early in the morning, stooping over with their
baskets—living bend-overs. At the ends of the rows, they
filled tubs with still-hard tomatoes and loaded them into a
pickup truck. Wendy remembered the children snatching
treats from the driver—candy or oranges. The oranges made
her sad. In Florida oranges were hardly a treat.

She still thought about the fields that ran to the horizon,
the dying vines exposing the rotting fruit, the clutch of
shacks at the border of the fields, the migrants playing cards
on citrus crates by the roadside. Even now, when she bought
vegetables, she found herself examining her hands and thinking of the workers' hands, scabby from the pesticides.

Her Florida boyfriend had been vituperative and paranoid,
always seething about slime-balls and bastards everywhere.
So now she was back, maybe romanticizing her memories of
home, embracing what she had once rejected as provincial.
She wondered if this was a case of reverse snobbery, or if it
was another phase that would dissolve into something else.
Bob Jackson, who managed a hardware store, was like a test
case. He didn't read much, except outdoor magazines. He
had never heard of inverted yield curves or fractals. He had
never listened to Pink Floyd until she showed him the video
of the Pompeii concert. He seemed to like it. He was one of
those guys who drove a pickup truck and wore a cap that was
likely to say "Big Snapper" or "John Deere" on the front.
She used to call good old boys GOBs, but now the acronym
seemed as appalling as a racial slur. She thought she had long
ago gotten away from men who got wrecked on beer every
weekend. But Bob intrigued her. It was true that he drank a
lot of beer, but he didn't have a beer belly, and somewhere
he had learned not to be boorish. One night recently they
had been walking from a shopping strip across a street to

where they had parked. A large sixties-vintage car crammed with guys holding their six-packs like lap dogs pulled out of a gas station. From an open window in the back, one of the men yelled at Wendy, "Hey, honey! Let's get naked and *spit*!" She burst out laughing. She was surprised that Bob laughed too. He didn't bristle. The car disappeared, and he was still laughing with her.

The furniture in Bob's chalet was Early American, all matching and new. He said he had ordered everything in one phone call, including some wall plaques of brass ducks in flight. Wendy examined Bob's trophy and listened to fish stories. In mid-April, when the crappie ran to the shallows to spawn, he had spent several days at the lake, fishing in the annual crappiethon. His freezer was full of fish, and now he fried some crappie and microwaved frozen store-bought hush puppies and french fries. After supper he showed her some snapshots he'd taken at the lake during the spring.

"Back in April, something happened out here that spooked me," he said, pausing over a shot of a sunset. "I woke up and thought I heard somebody crying—like a kitten stranded up in a tree. I looked up through the skylight. The trees had budded but hadn't leaved out yet. There was a bunch of bats out there, jumping around through the trees. Maybe this little noise was bats, but I thought bats squeaked at some high range humans can't pick up. I was half asleep and I'd been dreaming about being in a boat race—I guess I was excited and tense about the crappie run. I kept hearing it. It was an animal I'd never heard before. It was like a bird but sort of like a baby. I've been outdoors all my life, hunting and fishing, and I've *never* heard anything like that."

"At night your imagination seems to take over, doesn't it?"

He shook his head. "It was weird—like that Pink Floyd of

yours," he said, pulling at the raveling on the edge of his cut-offs.

"But you like Pink Floyd," she said with a laugh. "So they're yours too!"

Her eyes hit on the fish mounted on the wall. It was a twenty-pound catfish, in a pose of struggle. Beneath it, on a table, was a picture of Bob's son, a blond boy in a baseball cap reaching up eagerly to something out of camera range, like a dog about to jump up for a stick. Once, at a produce stand in Florida, near the migrants' shacks, Wendy had seen a little boy taunting a rooster, having a mock fight with it over a crust of bread. The rooster suddenly pecked a scab off the child's knee. The boy didn't cry. He just gazed in surprise at the blood trickling down his leg.

That night Wendy slept fitfully, and when she found herself fully awake, she realized she had been listening, in her sleep, for the unusual animal Bob had heard. An echo of a dream drifted around in her mind. She saw a bat cross the skylight. Bob had said he saw the bats jumping around, and she wondered if the word "bat" derived from "acrobat." It seemed odd that she had never thought of that before. Bob was snuffling a polite little snore. She could feel his body radiating heat. She eased out of bed and went to sit by the living room window. It was a moonlit night, and the landscape was washed silver with a dark backdrop of trees. The window had reflective glass; nothing could see in, but she could see out. That was true for daytime, but she wasn't sure about night. She imagined peeking in at their lives here in a few years—if they ended up together. He was vague about his ex-wife and the little boy, Todd, and Wendy suspected he wasn't over the marriage. Love frightened her. It seemed so arbitrary—a temporary madness, a blurring of perception.

She saw her eight years in Florida as a peculiar interlude, as if she had been wafting through the future like one of those parasailors she had seen riding through the sky on a parachute behind a motorboat. Sometimes in Florida she had suddenly asked herself, "*Who* do you think you are?" It struck her as unnatural and wrong that she—a small-town girl whose earliest ambition was to be a veterinarian—should be working on the twentieth floor of an icy air-conditioned building in one-hundred-degree weather. Now she looked back at her time in the corporate world as an aberration—like her schooling, an adolescent stage. Reading Marx or Camus was something you might do in college, when you're trying out possibilities, but not later, as an adult.

A faint hum entered her thoughts, growing until she realized she was hearing an airplane. A dog howled, far away. The plane was coming closer, and a light appeared, but in a moment the light blinked out. The engine seemed to quit. And then she heard—not a crash, but the plane's wheels whooshing fast on asphalt. Then the engine roared again. The plane had landed on the airstrip beyond the A-frame just ahead, and just as suddenly it was taking off. It passed so near the house she could see the outline of the wings, like some shadowy prehistoric bird. She followed the sound, and soon the red winking light appeared again. It faded out beyond the trees, and in a moment she heard a vehicle crunching on the gravel road down by the marina.

She darted up the stairs to the bedroom. "Something's happening," she said, shaking Bob.

He woke up easily. "What? What's wrong?"

"A plane landed but didn't stop. It cut its engines and its lights and just glided in and then took off. Then I heard a truck or something."

He staggered out of bed to look out the window. "There's nothing there now," she said, as they stood in front of the window, both nearly naked.

"Crazy fool," he said, shaking the sleep from his eyes. "This happened once before, back in April."

"The airstrip's not even finished, is it?"

"No. And it wasn't nothing but dirt back then."

"Remember how kids used to drag-race at the old airport late at night?"

"Yeah. I used to do that." They stood there for a moment, touching each other. He said, "A buddy of mine was driving to Atlanta once, and he passed some airport—Charlotte, North Carolina, I think. All of a sudden there was this plane landing right beside him. The runway was parallel to the road. He looked over and, by God, it was *Air Force One*—landing! But the funny thing was, it just touched down and took off again, like that plane just now." He spoke enthusiastically, running his hand through his hair like a cat suddenly licking its shoulder.

Wendy woke up at first light, made coffee, and took a mug out to the patio, sliding the glass door quietly. The air felt like rain, but she knew it was only the early-morning haze. The birds were singing—a loud, earnest congregation. She had forgotten to bring her bird book.

"Did you get back to sleep O.K.?" Bob called down from the balcony.

"Mmmm."

"Not too jangled?"

"No. It was just odd."

"I'd say it was probably somebody picking up a load of marijuana, but it's too early in the season."

With a mug of coffee, he joined her on the patio. There were wrinkled-sheet prints etched on his cheek. He said, "I dreamed I was taking flying lessons, and now that I'm awake I realize that's exactly what I want to do."

"What? Fly?"

"I guess so. The dream must have brought it out in me." He laughed at himself for some reason. He scooted his chair backwards, scraping the bricks. A nearby robin hopped across the grass. "When they started building that airstrip I started thinking about how nice it would be to taxi right up to the front door. And now I'm thinking—by God, why not? I can afford it." He rubbed the sleep out of his eyes. "Come on, coffee," he said. "Do your job."

"Won't it bother you, having all those planes buzzing over your house when the airstrip is finished?" she asked.

He shrugged. "It's just one of those things. Progress. I don't think I'd ever get bored watching airplanes."

"I meant the noise."

He laughed and tweaked her knee. "Airplanes make noise, Wendy. What do you expect?"

Late in the afternoon Bob's friends Jerry and Kim arrived in a junky Silverado. They were drinking cans of Coors.

"I'm afraid my mother's having some kind of break-down," Kim said as she set her can on a patio table. "She called me from St. Louis this morning in tears. It just didn't sound like Mother."

"Kim always has to have something to worry about," Jerry said, belching.

"I'm Wendy," said Wendy.

"Nice to meet you," Kim and Jerry said simultaneously.

"Has Bob been talking you to death with his fish stories?" Jerry teased.

"No, but he's been feeding me plenty of those crap-pie he caught this spring," said Wendy with a forced smile. She instantly disliked Jerry's loud personality and his beer gut, which was like a pregnancy with the baby carried high. Wendy wondered if people got louder as they gained weight.

Jerry guffawed. "He's feeding you plenty of crap, not crappie!"

Bob said, "Come on, Jerry, I need some help here. Don't go giving Wendy the wrong ideas about me."

Kim and Jerry were sunburned and oily, after a day out water-skiing with a borrowed motorboat. On the patio, where they gathered with some more beers, Jerry rubbed sunburn cream on Kim's back. Her swimsuit straps dangled down, revealing white stripes. She had one of those boyish haircuts that had been in style several years before. It was less than half an inch long all over and moussed to look bristly. Wendy thought it looked good on Kim.

When Bob told Kim and Jerry about the airplane landing in the night, Jerry said, "I imagine it was a drug drop-off from Colombia."

"Really?" Wendy was startled.

"We're not as out of touch here as people think," he said. "We're big-time."

"There's still a lot of cocaine coming up here," said Kim. "Bob, have you got any scissors? I'm going to whack that raveling off your shorts. It's driving me crazy."

Kim snipped the threads off Bob's shorts, and when she pulled some of the hairs on his leg he joked that he couldn't afford her haircut prices. It would not have occurred to Wendy to cut off those threads. She plunged a chip into a bowl of salsa Bob had set on a stool next to his boom box, which was going full-blast.

"I thought moving back here would be like moving back in time," Wendy said. She moved a wad of wet towels from a plastic chair.

"There's a lot of meanness around nowadays," Kim said. "I don't mean just children murdering each other at school."

"All that, and the law's still worried about potheads," Jerry said. "The sheriff's office is full of pictures of marijuana plants he's pulled out of people's cornfields."

"And probably took home to cure for himself!" said Kim.

Jerry and Kim were like a cross-talk act, jabbering at Wendy in a way that was hard for her to follow. Each seemed to be trying to outdo the other as they proceeded to report the details of their water-skiing adventures that afternoon. Wendy stepped over a pack of curl-tail plastic worms and Bob's crappie rig, a special pole with hooks spaced two feet apart. She could imagine fish lined up to feed on the pole like piglets at a sow. She followed Bob through the bright reflections on the sliding glass door, into the kitchen. He had told her he couldn't have survived the trauma of his divorce if it hadn't been for Jerry's friendship. Wendy couldn't imagine how that went.

The salad bowl contained screws and nails and flashlight batteries. Bob emptied it into a paper sack and began washing the bowl.

"Is it true? I mean about the cocaine?" Wendy asked.

"Who knows?" He rinsed the bowl and shook the water from it. "Remember the bananas? All the bananas used to come up here from New Orleans on the train and they'd get unloaded in Fulton, and then get shipped in all directions, all over the country. I think it's like that—a central location."

"The heartland," she suggested.

"Whatever that means."

"Do they still have the banana festival every year?"

"Yeah. The world's biggest banana pudding gets bigger every year. But it's like everything else nowadays, just something that's supposed to remind you of how things used to be."

She dried the bowl. "I wish I had some banana pudding like my grandmother used to make."

"You've been away too long, Wendy."

"I guess," she said idly.

Bob backed her up against a broom in the corner between the refrigerator and the open hall door. He said with a grin, "Do you think it could be any easier with us than it is with most people?"

"I don't know," she murmured. "It looks easy. But I'm afraid it's not."

"I'm scared too," he said abruptly.

Kim walked in on their embrace but didn't seem to notice. She disappeared into the bathroom. Wendy could see Jerry out on the patio fooling with a fishing rod, casting out across the grass and reeling in a large wad of plastic trash.

The day's heat had accumulated in a stuffy gauze over the sky, and the light was washing out. Wendy and Kim followed a trail through the marsh, where a green heron was poking about in the shallows. Lily pads—double-deckers the size of serving trays, with colossal blossoms—carpeted the edge of the water. A woodcock flew overhead. Shafts of dusty light blazed through the dim woods. Wendy peered ahead, trying to spot the nineteenth-century iron furnace she knew was beyond the marsh.

"Don't you miss it down in Florida?" asked Kim, slapping at a bug on her leg.

Wendy hesitated. "In a way. But I'd rather be here now. It seems different here now. Houses I used to dislike seem charming. But that's O.K. I'm the one that's changed, not the houses."

"My dream house is going to have one of those Florida rooms," Kim said. "But I may never get out of a double-wide."

She brushed a spiderweb from her arm. She had on blue shorts and a white blouse she had pulled over her swimsuit. The top of her suit was dark through the blouse. Wendy imagined having a sunburn—warm, like passion, against her clothes. Last night her skin had felt like that, with Bob's hot body asleep next to her. For a dreamy moment now she thought about sex, looking forward to it again that night. She paused to pick up the gray dried center of one of last season's pond lilies. It was shaped like a showerhead.

"In the fall there's a blue zillion of those here," said Kim. "But in a gift shop you'd pay two bucks for one." She examined the ground. "Bob really likes you, Wendy," she said suddenly.

"Do you think so?" Wendy dropped the dried lily. "I can't tell how he really feels about me."

"He's hard to know, but if he decides to be your friend, then he's your friend for life. That's why his divorce was so hard on him. But she took him to the cleaners—she carried every stick of furniture with her to Minnesota."

"He told me this morning he wants to learn to fly an airplane. Maybe he wants to fly to Minnesota."

"I don't know. He's done a lot of neat stuff—challenge-type stuff. Did you know he used to work for a guy that called himself a swamp specialist? They'd put on waders and just march out into the swamp and collect snakes and weeds and things for the university."

The fading light was eerie, and mosquitoes were materializing from the thick air. Wendy gazed out over the water—patched with debris and plants and dappled light. The place seemed inviting. She had a pleasant image in her mind of that swamp specialist—a man in love with the murky deeps, like Jacques Cousteau.

Bob was serious about learning to fly. He began taking lessons the following weekend and for the next several weeks buried himself in instruction manuals. Wendy came out to the lake each Saturday. She found it peculiar that a small event, at secondhand report, could spur an ambition like flying and that it could possibly make your life turn a corner. The desire to fly must come from a romantic temperament, she thought—a fundamental rebellion against gravity itself—but the *ability* to fly required a single-mindedness, and a calm, almost mundane focus. It was a contradiction explained only by arrogance, she decided. When she watched Bob aim his motorboat out of the shallows into the open water, she could easily imagine him flying. He was nervous when he wasn't using his body, as if his mind had lost its anchor.

At the airport one Saturday afternoon, she watched the Cessna come in for the landing, wobbling and jerking. She could see Bob beside the instructor, and he seemed to be concentrating hard. The plane touched down, scooted along briefly, then lifted off again like a cat being chased up a tree.

When the plane landed again, he jumped out and rushed toward her. "Did you see us doing touch-and-go's?" he cried, grabbing her by the shoulders.

"Yeah, like that plane I heard that time."

"I'll be ready to solo by the end of the summer!" he said. "Then I'll fly you to the moon, or wherever you want to go." He laughed as he shed his light jacket. "Paducah maybe?"

Wendy was drifting with the summer, suspended, but knowing that summers always end too soon, like delicious dreams. On a hot Saturday evening in August, Kim and Jerry came out again. Wendy had forgotten how shrill their voices were. She went into the kitchen from the patio to get a beer. Searching for something to pour it into, she found a slim, ridged glass she liked. She could see the others out on the patio, their loud laughter slapping the air. Jerry's voice

climbed above the rest—"He'll go crying home to Mama
if they repossess his car." In the lowering light, the heat
of Kim's dark tan was deepening, flushing her face. Bob,
grilling steaks, was clad only in a barbecue mitt and a narrow
red swimsuit that fit like an Ace bandage. He shed the mitt
and headed toward the reflective-glass doors like a bird cap-
tivated by the illusion of sky.

He came inside then and pulled a wad of loose paper napkins from a drawer. They had been crammed between some
appliance manuals and what looked like paired socks. He
said, "Jerry wants us all to go down to Mud Island next
weekend. You want to go? It might be fun."

"But Kim said she was going to St. Louis to see her
mother." Wendy turned away from Bob, not wanting to
admit how the thought of a trip with Jerry and Kim gave her
the heebie-jeebies, but she knew he caught her tone.

Bob's hand on her shoulder twisted her around. "Do you
want to go some other time? Just you and me?"

"If you really want me to."

"I just now invited you, didn't I?" Holding her arm
against the refrigerator, he talked straight into her eyes. "If I
ask you to go to Mud Island with me, I mean go to Mud Island with me."

"I'm sorry," she said, embarrassed. "I just feel out of
place."

"Do you think you're too good for my friends?"

She looked away. "I just don't think Jerry treats Kim with
much respect," she said, although that wasn't all of it.

"There's more history there than you see," said Bob.
"You just don't know them." He whipped the steak sauce
from the counter, and she followed him out. He said, "Half
the time I feel like I'm apologizing for the human race, and
half the time I feel like there's been some mistake—why

wasn't I born a catfish or a tree?" He laughed, but with little humor. "Nobody ever feels they belong, you know that?" He started spearing steaks. "And everybody has to feel they're superior to somebody. It stinks."

Jerry and Kim stopped talking, whatever they were saying. "What's that all about?" they said to each other.

"Y'all get your butts in gear," said Bob briskly. "Everybody grab a plate."

It would be dark soon. The mosquitoes weren't bad. Bob had lighted some buckets of citronella. A rock station was playing Pearl Jam, the music disappearing under the talk-show gab of a million crickets. Something shifted in the evening as the light dimmed, as if they all felt safer now with one another, their awkward judgments and hesitations erased as their faces grew indistinct. Although Wendy still smarted, she was enjoying the languorous evening, the slow buildup of desire. The heat felt subtropical. Occasionally something unidentifiable pattered down from the leaves on the redbud tree.

As they were finishing the meal, a pair of headlights approached. A truck door slammed and Bob crossed the yard to speak to the driver. Wendy heard murmurs and the rise and fall of urgent talk. The truck roared off, and Bob hurried back.

"A little girl's lost," he called. "We have to go look for her."

Wendy grasped for details. Bob quickly explained that it was one of the Smith children who lived a few houses up the road. She had been playing in the backyard after supper. "Her mother thought the boy was watching her, and the boy thought his mother was watching her, so she slipped out of sight."

"How long ago?" Jerry said.

"Not long. They reckon she wandered off in the woods. They didn't hear any cars come up."

The tone of the evening shifted again. Wendy ran to the bathroom and grabbed some Kleenex and mosquito repellent. Sorrow descended in her like water whirling down a drain. Bob emerged from the house in jeans, with a flashlight and a T-shirt he pulled on as he walked.

"This is the kind of thing that makes me never want to have a kid," Kim said angrily. She snapped open a fresh can of beer.

"We'll never find her in the dark," Jerry said.

"Well, we have to try," Bob said. "I know which one they're talking about—Marlie. She's a cute little girl. She's about four."

On foot, they set out along the inlet. Kim and Jerry split off down the road that branched toward some houses and a small section of woods. Wendy and Bob headed toward the marina.

"Marlie!" Bob bellowed into the twilight.

They could see the wide-open point of land ahead, beyond the marina, with a few stark pine trees rimming the shore. A small road led up to some picnic tables. Bob was walking so fast Wendy had to take two steps for each one of his. They saw no sign of a child, no scrap of clothing or toy, no TV clichés. The point was deserted.

"This is impossible," Bob said, kicking at a log.

"Listen." Wendy cupped her ear. "No, it's nothing." She called out the child's name.

They followed the road that joined the airstrip. They could see across the marsh to some lights on houseboats moored around the point.

"Man, what kids can do to you—it's a crime!" Bob said. "This is the hatefulest thing."

"Maybe Kim's right," said Wendy. "Perverts, guns, leukemia—think of the problems kids bring."

"Ex-wives with a grudge. Add that to your list."

"Someday you'll tell me more about that," she said, reaching her arm around his waist as they walked.

He slowed his pace and waited a minute to speak. "Todd, my boy, ran away once, and it scared us to death. I panicked and ran all over the neighborhood, and up the railroad track. Come to find out, he had wandered down to a neighbor's. But they get out of your sight, and you're just helpless."

"You must feel that way now, since he's literally out of your sight."

"You know the last time I saw him? It's been a year and a half."

"That's awful!"

"He was eight years old. He would be nearly ten now."

"That's what you say when they're dead—he *would be.*"

"It's like he's dead in some way."

"Why don't you go see him?"

Bob didn't answer right away. The night was quiet. The water lapping on the boats at the marina was still faintly audible. He said, "It wasn't any big fight or anything. She just up and left."

"You've got a right to see him."

"I guess. I don't know. It's too humiliating. He won't know me."

Wendy shook herself loose from him and stopped. She said, "Look, I don't know why you're so passive about him— or about me. You're totally *un*passive in other things—your boat, fishing, flying. You're a guy who *does* things. So why don't you *do* something about this? Go with Kim and Jerry to Mud Island? What is the point? I want to go to Mud Island about like I want to go to Disney World."

"Shhh. Don't get onto me. I can't help it. Here, don't get upset, please." He wound his arm around her shoulder again.

She would have cried, but she wasn't sure how involved she was in this moment, whether the lost child had really penetrated her consciousness. The news was so sudden; it was like being catapulted out of bed by an earthquake.

"Let's go back," he said, with a sigh like a truck releasing its brake.

After they reached the house, they drove up to the Smith place to see what was going on, but there was no news. Wendy sat in the car while Bob got out and talked to a policeman and a neighbor. The policeman's flashing lights made Wendy think of a carnival. When Bob returned to the car, he said, "Bill Kilmer's bringing a searchlight and we're going to get the boat out. He's going to meet me at the house."

Wendy stood on the patio. It was dark now, and the insects were singing loudly. Bob took a load of dishes inside, pushing the sliding door shut with his foot. She saw him raking scraps into the sack under the sink and rinsing off the plates. It dawned on her that of course you could see through reflective glass at night if the light was on. It seemed naïve of her to have wondered about that before—ages ago. When Bob came outside, he steered her by the shoulder until they were away from the lights. The moon was up. There was a glow where the moon was shining on a cloud bank, and high up some stars had popped out. Just above, among the highest trees, the bats were taking off.

"Look how they fly," Bob said. "They don't fly like birds, because they're unstable. An airplane or a bird has stability. Birds soar and use their bodies to fly through the air, but bats, with that sonar they've got, are always jerking around, bouncing off walls of sound. Look how fast their wings flutter."

"They're jitterbugging," said Wendy, tugging at his waist, pulling him into a slow, sensuous dance.

They both laughed quietly—something tentatively shared. As they danced, a faster song came on the radio and they adjusted to the quicker pace. Then Jerry and Kim appeared and joined in, babbling like strange animals. Now they were all jitterbugging like bats across the moon, as if that was all anybody could do under the circumstances.

Charger

As he drove to the shopping center, Charger rehearsed how he was going to persuade his girlfriend, Tiffany Marie Sanderson, to get him some of her aunt Paula's Prozac. He just wanted to try it, to see if it was right for him. Tiffany hadn't taken him seriously when he had mentioned it before. "Don't you like to try new things?" he asked her. He would try anything, except unconventional food. But she seemed more interested in redecorating her room than in revamping her mind.

He cruised past the fast-food strip, veered into the left-turn lane, and stopped at the light. He stared at the red arrow like a cat waiting to pounce. He made the turn and scooted into a good spot in the shopping-center parking lot. At the drink machines in front of the home-fashions store where Tiffany worked after school, he reached into his work pants for a couple of quarters. He needed to wash himself out. He felt contaminated from the chemicals at work. He fed the quarters into a machine, randomly selecting the drink he would have chosen anyway—the Classic. He wondered if there was any freedom of choice about anything. Tiffany wanted to get married in June, right after her graduation. He had not proposed, exactly, but the idea had grown. He was uneasy about it. His mother said he was too young to marry—nineteen, a baby. She pointed out that he could barely make his truck payments and said Tiffany would expect new furniture and a washer and dryer. And Charger knew that Tiffany's fat-assed father disapproved of him. He said Charger was the type of person who would fall through the cracks when he found out he couldn't rely on his goofy charm to keep him out of trouble. Tiffany's father called it "riding on your face." Charger was inclined to take that as a compliment. He believed you had to use your natural skills to straddle the cracks of life if you were going to get anywhere at all. Apparently he gave the impression that he wasn't ready for anything—like a person half dressed who suddenly finds himself crossing the street. Yet he was *not* a fuck-up, he insisted to himself.

Tiffany appeared in front of the store, a bright smile spreading across her face. She wore tight little layers of slinky black. She had her hair wadded up high on her head like a squirrel's nest, with spangles hanging all over it. She had on streaks of pink makeup and heavy black eyebrows applied like pressure-sensitive stickers. She was gorgeous.

"Hi, babe," she said, squinching her lips in an air kiss.

"Hi, beautiful," Charger said. "Want something to drink?" Then she raised her hand and he saw the bandage on her thumb. "Hey, what happened?" he asked, touching her hand.

"I mashed my thumb in the drill press in shop."

"Holy shit! You drilled a hole in your thumb?"

"No. It's just a bruise. It's not as bad as it looks."

"How did it happen?" He held her hand, but she pulled it away from him.

"I was holding a piece of wood for Tammy Watkins? And we were yakking away, and I had my thumb in too far, and she brought the drill press right down on my thumb. But not the drill, just the press part."

"I bet that *hurt.* Does it still hurt?"

"It's O.K. I'm just lucky I didn't lose my dumb thumb."

As they walked down the sidewalk, she repeated the details of her accident. He gulped some Coke. His stomach burned. He could hardly bear to listen as he imagined the drill press crunching her thumb. He whistled in that ridiculous way one does on learning something astounding. Then he whistled again, just to hear the sound. It blotted out the image of the drill going through her thumb.

"I might lose my thumbnail, but it'll grow in again," Tiffany said.

"I wish I could kiss it and make it all better," he said. His throat ached, and he itched.

"No problem," she said. "Didn't you ever mash a finger with a hammer?"

"Yeah. One time when I was cracking hickory nuts."

A young couple carrying a baby in a plastic cradle emerged from the pizza place. The woman was mumbling something about rights. The man said, "I don't give a damn what you do. *Go* to Paducah for all I care."

Charger guided Tiffany by the elbow through the traffic into the parking lot. She said, "I asked Aunt Paula about her pills, and she said I didn't need one." Tiffany swung her bandaged hand awkwardly in his direction, as if she were practicing a karate move. She laughed. "And I can't open her pill bottle and sneak one out with this thing on my thumb."

"It looks like a little Kotex," he said.

She giggled. "Not exactly. How would you know?"

"Did you tell Paula the pill was for me?"

"No." Her voice shifted into exasperation. "If you want one, go ask her yourself."

"Man, I gotta get me one of those pills." He struck a theatrical pose, flinging the back of his hand against his forehead. "I'm so depressed, I'm liable to just set down right here in the parking lot and melt into that spot of gop over there. I get depressed easy." He snapped his fingers. "I go down just like that."

They reached his truck, and he slammed his hands on the hot hood. Then he realized that Tiffany was holding up her thumb like a hitchhiker, waiting for him to open the door for her. She said, "Charger, you're not depressed. I don't believe that. It's just something you've heard on TV."

"When do I hear TV? I don't even watch it." They were talking across the hood.

"*I* don't get depressed," said Tiffany. Her hair seemed to lift like wings, along with her spirit. "I always say, if I've got my lipstick on, nothing else matters."

"I know, Miss Sunshine."

"Why would you get depressed anyway? You've got a decent job at the bomb plant. You've got a truck with floating blue lights. You've got a fiancée—me. You've got nothing to complain about."

Charger didn't answer. Stepping around to her side, he opened her door and boosted her in. The fun of having a high-rider was helping girls in, cupping their rear pears in his eager paws. Yet he had not tried out this automotive technique on many girls, because he started going with Tiffany soon after he bought the truck. She always squealed with pleasure when he heaved her in. Charger had fallen for Tiffany when she stole the YARD OF THE MONTH sign from someone's yard and ran naked with it down the street at midnight. He had dared her to do it, while he waited in his truck at the end of the street. It was a street where big dudes lived, people who spent piles of money on yard decorators and had swimming pools behind fences. Now he loved her, probably, and he wanted to have sex with her every day, but he had trouble telling her his deepest thoughts. He didn't want her to laugh at him. He wasn't sure he *was* depressed, but he was curious about Prozac. It was all the rage. He had heard it was supposed to rewire the brain. That idea intrigued him. He liked the sound of it too—Prozac, like some professional athlete named Zack. "Hi, I'm Zack. And I'm a pro. I'm a pro at everything I do. Just call me Pro Zack."

Tiffany had told him that her aunt Paula took Prozac because she was worried about her eyelids bagging. Her insurance wouldn't cover a facelift or an eye tuck, but it would pay for anti-depressants if she was depressed about her face—or about her health coverage. Prozac seemed to give her a charge of self-esteem, so that she could live with her baggy eyes. "I feel good about myself," Paula was fond of announcing now.

That was what Charger was interested in, a shift of attitude. Bad moods scared him. He didn't know where they came from. Sometimes he just spit at the world and roared around like a demon in his truck, full of meanness. He had actually kicked at his father's dog, and the other day he deliberately dropped his mother's Christmas cactus, still wrapped in its florist's foil. His father had disappeared in December, and now it was May. Months passed before they heard from him. His mother pretended indifference. She didn't even call the police or report him missing. "He'll come back with his tail between his legs," she said. Charger believed that she knew where his father was and just didn't want him to know.

Charger answered the telephone when his father finally

called, in April, from Texas. He had left the day before Christmas and just kept driving; once he got out of Kentucky, he couldn't turn back, he said. Might as well see what there is to see, he said. He hadn't had a chance to call, and he knew Charger's mother wouldn't worry about him.

"Are you coming back?" Charger wanted to know.

"Depends on what the future holds," his father said vaguely.

"What do you mean by that?" Charger said, thinking that his father wouldn't be happy even if he did come back. He realized how sad-faced and thin his dad had been. He was probably having a better time where he was, out looking at skies. "I never knew about skies before," his dad had said in a mysteriously melancholy voice. He started singing a song, as if the telephone were a microphone and he had grabbed a stage opportunity. "Ole buttermilk sky, can't you see my little donkey and me, we're as happy as a Christmas tree." In a hundred years, Charger would not have imagined his dad bursting into song.

Charger sometimes looked at his life as if he were a spy peering through a telescope. The next afternoon he could see himself and Tiffany as though he were watching from the other side of town. He saw a carefree young couple frolicking at Wal-Mart together. At least, that was how he tried to picture himself with Tiffany—as beautiful people in a commercial, scooting around having fun. They played hide-and-go-seek in the maze of tall aisles, piled to the ceiling with goods. He whistled "Buttermilk Sky," and she followed the sound from aisle to aisle. She caught him in lingerie, where the canyons of housewares gave way to prairies of delicate flowers.

"I win!" she cried, taunting him with a pair of pink panties on a hanger.

A country-western star was at the store that day, signing pictures to promote his new album. He was a young heart-throb named Andy or Randy something. He was sitting at a table next to a shopping cart full of his CDs. Charger didn't trust the guy. His shirt was too fancy.

"Bet he didn't buy them duds here," Charger said to Tiffany.

"He doesn't have to," Tiffany said, her breath trailing like gauze. "Oh, I've *got* to get his autograph."

Charger stood waiting in line with Tiffany, feeling ridiculous. Tiffany had on snake pants. Her legs looked like two sensational boa constrictors. They were attracting comments. A woman and a little girl were standing in line behind Charger and Tiffany. The woman—overdressed in beads and floral fabric—was eyeing Tiffany.

"She's going on his tour," Charger told the woman impulsively. "She's a singer."

"Oh," the woman gasped. "Do you know him?"

"Yes, as a matter of fact," Charger told the woman. He felt his orneriness kicking in. He couldn't help himself when opportunities like this arose. "We're in his entourage. What do you need to know about country's newest sensation, Randy what's-his-name?"

"Andy," Tiffany said, elbowing him.

The woman said, "I'm a lounge pianist and former gospel artist? I've been trying for months to get my tapes to Andy." She had the tapes in her hand. "I know he'd love them. Our hearts are on the same wavelength. His songs tell my life story." She jerked her head to the left. "Get back here, Reba," she yelled to the little girl, who had spun off down the cosmetics aisle. She reeled the child in and continued at some length. She said her life was a Barbara Mandrell kind of story, involving a car wreck and a comeback. The woman wore a country-music hairdo—a mountain of frizz and fluff that looked to Charger as though it had sprung out of a jack-in-the-box.

A number of young girls in the line—pre-babe material, Charger thought—had long frizzed and fluffed hair too.

"Your story is an inspiration," Charger said to the woman. Tiffany whispered to Charger, "You're embarrassing me." The gospel-lounge singer heard and frowned at Tiffany. Charger imagined the woman sticking out her tongue.

Charger said, "If you give me your name and number, I'll have you on television inside a month."

"Here's my card," the woman said. "You'll put in a word to him about my tapes, won't you?" She took her child's hand. "Come on, Reba. Stay in this line or I'm going to skin your butt."

The little girl clutched one of Andy's CDs and a box of hamster food.

"I like hamsters. I had hamster for supper last night," Charger said, making a face at the child.

Tiffany made the same face at Charger. "Why do you do things like that?" she said. "It irks me."

"Irk? I *irk*? Well, pardon me all over the place." He flapped his arms like a bird. *"Irk. Irk."* Teasingly, he nudged Tiffany with his knee, and then he pinched her on the rear end. "I'm a hawk. *Irk.*"

"Cool."

Afterward, as they drove out of the crowded parking lot, Tiffany was engrossed in her autographed picture of the cowboy warbler. As she traced her finger along the signature, her bandaged thumb seemed to erase his face. She had grown quiet when it was her turn to meet the star. She had said to him, "All I can say is, 'Wow.' "

"He probably never heard anything so stupid," she said

now, as Charger turned onto the main drag. "I was so excited I couldn't think of what to say!"

"I'm sure what you said is exactly what he wanted to hear," Charger said. "He eats it up. Isn't he from Atlanta? He probably thinks we're just dumb hicks here."

Tiffany said excitedly, "Oh, let's go to Atlanta this weekend."

"And blow my paycheck?"

"We can manage."

Charger braked at the red light. He stared at Tiffany as if he had just picked up a hitchhiker. Sometimes he felt he didn't know her at all. Her snake legs squirmed—impatient to shed their skins, he thought.

On Friday after work Charger decided to go straight to the source. He thought that Tiffany's aunt might give him some of her Prozac if he caught her in the right mood. Paula was O.K. She covered for them when Tiffany spent the night with him. Paula said that her sister, Tiffany's mother, would die if she knew about the little overnight trips in Charger's truck.

Paula hadn't expected him, but she seemed pleased to see him at the door. She brought him through the living room into the kitchen. "Don't look at this garbage," she said.

She had school projects—flags and Uncle Sam dolls and Paul Revere hats—scattered around. She taught fourth grade.

Charger noticed that her eyelids drooped down onto her eyelashes, but her face had few wrinkles. He wondered how long Tiffany's eyelids would hold up. She resembled her aunt—the same smidgen nose and whirlpool curls.

Paula handed him a glass of ice and a two-liter Coke. He poured, and the Coke foamed over onto the kitchen counter.

He sat numbly on a stool, embarrassed. While she wiped up the spill, she said, "This morning I dressed in the dark and put on one blue sock and one green sock?" She laughed. "At school I got a citation for a fashion violation. At school we get citations for bad hair, static cling, leopard-skin underwear beneath white pants, color clash, sock displacement. The fashion police sentenced me to work in the beehive section of the fashion salon."

"You've still got on a blue sock and a green sock," Charger said. He wondered how her fourth-graders dealt with her high-pitched babbling.

"Do you want a mayonnaise sandwich?" she asked.

"No. Do you eat kid food, being's you're a teacher?"

"I have to have at least a teaspoon of Miracle Whip a day or I'll blow my brains out," she said. "Bill won't eat anything at lunch but crackers. I get mad at him because he won't eat the food I leave for him. He won't eat fruits and vegetables. I said, 'There are some grapes on the counter.' He said, 'Are they washed?' I said no. He said, 'I don't have to wash crackers.' But he's sure slim and trim on the cracker diet. I'll give him that."

"Give that man a Twinkie!" Charger said, jumping off the stool in what he thought was a dramatic gesture. "You don't have to wash Twinkies."

"I don't know if he ought to eat Twinkies."

"Well, if that don't work, give him a Ding Dong." He grinned.

"He's already got a ding-dong."

"Then give him a Little Debbie."

"But I don't want him to have a little Debbie."

Charger laughed. "Little Debbies are my favorite."

"Charger, you're such a great kidder." She laughed with him, shaking her head. "And you're such a baby."

When Charger finally got around to mentioning Paula's Prozac, she didn't seem surprised that he wanted to try the drug.

"I need to reprogram my head," he said.

"Why not go to church? Or take piano lessons?"

"Why don't *you?*"

Paula opened a cabinet above the toaster and chose a vial of pills. "You don't really need these pills, Charger. You just need to believe in yourself more."

"My *self* doesn't have that much to do with it."

"Maybe you just haven't found it yet. You've got a deep soul, Charger. Tiffany doesn't see it yet, but she will, in time."

She shook the pill bottle in his face like a baby rattle. She said, "One of the side effects of these little numbers is that they can make you nonorgasmic. But I've tested that thoroughly, and it's not true for me. I don't have that side effect!" She laughed loudly. "I don't think you want one of these, Charger."

"It might be just what I need to relax my sex machine. It's running away with me." He winked.

She turned serious. She put the pills back in the cabinet and said, "Charger, I believe you're scared. You don't act like you're ready to settle down and have a family. Have you given any thought to what you would do if you and Tiffany had a baby?"

"She's not pregnant, is she?" he asked, alarmed.

"Not that I know of. But it's something you have to be ready for."

He *had* thought about it. He wasn't ready for it. The idea was all wrong. Some guys he knew were working hard to feed their kids. They were not much older than he was, but they seemed years older. He couldn't imagine being a father yet. He knew he didn't have much chance of rising above the loading dock, at minimum wage. How could he feed a kid? He tried to shake off the thought. That was the distant future.

Charger and Tiffany didn't get away until after eight o'clock that night, after he had changed his oil and worked on his carburetor. They were going to Nashville instead of Atlanta. Tiffany's mother was having a family dinner on Sunday for Tiffany's cousin's birthday, and Tiffany had decided that Atlanta was too far away for them to get back in time. She said she wanted to go to a store in Nashville called Dangerous Threads.

On the drive Charger drank a can of beer. He glanced at Tiffany. She had on her snake pants again. They sort of gave him the creeps. He slid his hand down her thigh. The pants had a slinky, snaky feel that startled him every time he touched them. He moved his hand in little circles over her inner thigh. His hand moved like a computer mouse, tracing the snaky terrain beneath it.

"Do you think I've been acting funny?" Charger asked.

"No. Why?" She was picking at the closure on her bandage. It made a scratchy sound, like a mouse in a wall.

"You don't think I'm moody, or liable to jump up and say the wrong thing or throw a flowerpot on the floor? You're not scared to cross the state line with me? You don't think I'm weird?"

"No, I think you're just super-sexy. And you're fun-loving. I rate that real high." Twisting in her seat to reach him, she touched his cheek with her bandaged thumb. It was splinted for protection.

"What do you want to do in Nashville besides shop?" he asked.

"Go to that new mall, and maybe get into a good show at Opryland, and stay in a big hotel."

With her quick enthusiasm, she was like a child in Santa's lap. "Motel Six is more like it," he said.

"Well, that's all right. I just think we ought to have our fling before we get married and can't run around so much."

Charger was passing a long-haul truck. He returned to the right-hand lane. The truck was far behind, like an image in slow motion. "Let's go to Texas instead of Nashville," he said.

"It's too far. And we're headed in the wrong direction."

"We could drive straight through."

She didn't answer. In a moment she said, "If you're thinking about your daddy, you know you can't find him just by driving to Texas for the weekend."

"I know, but I wish I could." He glanced at the rearview for cops and chugged some beer. "When Daddy called from Texas this spring, I was about two french fries short of happy," he said. "And then the feeling just wound down, and I thought I could sort of see why he did what he did, and I could see me doing it too." He shuddered. "It gives me the bummers."

He was afraid Tiffany wasn't listening. She was pulling at a strand of her hair, twirling it around her finger. But then she said, "I was just thinking about your dad. I was wondering what he was doing out there. And why your mother didn't make more of a fuss about him going off."

"She was probably glad he was gone," Charger said. He belched loudly. *"Irk!"* he said, to be funny. He made her laugh.

They stopped for gas, then kept driving and driving. They sped past the Cracker Barrel. Usually they stopped there and ate about eight pounds of rosin-roasted potatoes and big slabs of ham. He so often overdid things, he thought sorrowfully. He had gotten his nickname years earlier from his childhood habit of charging into things without thinking.

Recently he had dared himself to drive up the bank side of the clay pit; he was trying out his new used truck. The road wound around the clay pit, ascending steeply on one side. The dirt was loose. He wasn't scared. He thought, I can do this. He steered very carefully and inched up the winding trail.

"I can do this," he said now, in a barely audible voice.

Tiffany patted his arm affectionately. She said, "Charger, I know you don't know what you want to do with your life. And you don't make a whole lot. But we have plenty of time. I know we're going to be real happy." She spoke as though she had worked that up in her mind for the past two hours. Then she switched gears again, back to her usual self. She said, "See the moon? I am just thrilled out of my mind to see that moon. I love seeing the moon. I love going to church. I love work. I love driving at night. I love getting sleepy and snuggling up to you."

The moon was rising, a pale disk like a contact lens. The bright lights in the other lane obscured the path in front of him. He hit his brights and could see again. The stretch of highway just ahead looked clean and clear. Tiffany made everything seem so simple—like his father bursting into song about sky-watching. Was love that easy?

He ran his hand along her leg, up the inseam. Then he turned on the radio. A song ended, followed by some unidentifiable yapping. He hit the SEEK button. Tiffany screeched. "That's Andy! Turn it up. I just love that voice of his."

"Personally, I think he's full of himself," Charger said.

"Oh, you just wish *you* could carry a tune." With her left hand she slapped her leg along with the song.

The singer sounded like a cranky old crow, Charger thought. It was an odd voice for such a young guy. Charger had no special talents. He had never had any encouragement from anybody in his life other than Tiffany. She wanted him to take a computer course, because everything was computers now. But he knew he couldn't sit still that long. That was the trouble with high school. He liked his present job at the bomb plant O.K., because he got to joke around with a bunch of people he enjoyed. He called it "the bomb plant" because it produced fertilizer. He felt lucky to have such an attractive girlfriend. But he was aware that his mother, too, had been cute when she was young. Now she was overweight and had a hacking cough. His father had worked at the tire plant for twenty-five years, and his mother was a nurse's aide at the hospital. She emptied bedpans. They lived in a tacky, cramped house that she took little pride in. They did not go on vacations. His father watched television every evening. He used to watch a regular lineup. But when they got cable and a remote, he couldn't stick to his old favorites. He cruised the airwaves, lighting here and there. Five afternoons a week Charger's mother cooked supper for the family, left it on the table, and went off to work. She grew heavy and tired from being on her feet long hours. She was forty-four years old. Her eyelids drooped, but she didn't even seem to know it. Maybe when Tiffany was that age, she would accept baggy eyes as gracefully as she regarded her injured thumb. He shuddered.

Driving down the interstate, Charger contemplated his life. He was nineteen years old and still lived with his mother, but already he was thinking ahead to the middle of his life. Since his father disappeared, Charger had been catapulted forward. Something about his mind wouldn't let him be young, he thought. He saw too far ahead. He wanted to rewire his brain. He wanted to plunge into the darkness and not be afraid. Being in love ought to seem more reckless, he thought. Tiffany was napping, her head nestled in a yellow pillow in the form of a giant Tweety Pie. It did not look like a comfortable position, but she seemed relaxed. Her snake legs were beautiful. They seemed almost to glow in the dark. When they reached Nashville, Charger impulsively turned down I-40 toward Memphis. He thought Tiffany wouldn't mind if they headed west. He felt like driving all night. He thought he could reach the Texas border sometime tomorrow. Then he could get his bearings. Tiffany kept sleeping, tired from school and work. He played the radio low, a background for his thoughts. He finished a Coke he had bought at the gas station. He had to keep his head open for the road. In the dark the road seemed connected to his head, like a tongue.

Just before two he pulled off the interstate at a cheap-looking motel. Tiffany woke up but didn't seem to notice where she was. He guided her into the lobby. Clumsily she struggled with her purse and the heavy satchel she had brought with her. Charger pressed a buzzer on the wall to awaken the night clerk. He could hear noises from the back room, like someone swatting flies. Tiffany studied her bandage as they waited at a pine-paneled counter. She squirmed restlessly. "I have to pee so bad," she said. Charger wondered how she wriggled out of those tight snake pants.

A thin middle-aged man in sweatpants and an oversized Charlotte Hornets jersey appeared. He wore thick glasses. Silently he took Charger's credit card and ground it through a little press. The man grunted as he presented the paper slip. The room was thirty-two dollars—less than Charger had feared. Pleased, he signed the slip with a grand flourish, as if he were endorsing an important document. The clerk ripped out the yellow copy, wrapped it around the key, and handed the little package to Charger.

"I'm going to get muscles in my left arm," Tiffany said as she hoisted her satchel. She held her bandaged thumb ahead of her, like a flashlight.

From the truck Charger retrieved the other bag she had brought and his own bag, a weathered Army duffel of his father's. The room was 234, up an exterior flight of concrete stairs. A light rain had started. Below, a car pulled in, and a woman got out with a screaming child clutching a pink-plush pig. Charger heard a door slam.

The room smelled stale. The bedspread looked heavy and dark with dirt and smoke and spills. Charger set the bags down and clicked on a light. Then the telephone rang. Tiffany gasped, but Charger thought it seemed normal to get a phone call here. He picked up the phone.

"Your Nellie-babe dropped a scarf on the floor down here," the night clerk said.

"You dropped your scarf," Charger said to Tiffany, who was tugging at her zipper. "I'll be right down," he told the clerk. He hung up the phone. Nellie-babe?

"Wait. I have to pee and I need a little help with these pants," Tiffany said, reaching for him. "I feel ham-handed."

"You can do it. How did you manage at that gas station?"

"Why I dropped my scarf is, I couldn't tie it around my neck with this clumsy thumb."

"I'll go get it." Charger slipped out of the room and bounded down to the desk, leaving Tiffany to work herself out of her snake pants. She whined when she was tired.

"Some britches your Nellie's got on," the night clerk said in a friendly voice.

"How am I supposed to take that?" Charger demanded. "And what do you mean—Nellie? Is that something I'm supposed to know from television?"

The skinny guy retreated an inch or two, and his lip quavered. Charger felt gratified. The clerk said, "Hey, man. I didn't mean nothing. I mean you're a lucky guy. No offense. I was just commenting on them snakes." He grinned. He had big teeth, chinked with food. "I mean, I wouldn't want to get tangled up with a lady wearing snakes. I looked at those, and they threw me for a minute. Man, I hate snakes. Did a snake bite her on the finger?"

Charger snatched Tiffany's scarf from the counter. It was a long banner, shimmering blue like a lava lamp. He went to the door and stood gazing at the parking lot. The winking motel sign had a faulty bulb. DUNN'S MOTEL. DUNN'S MOTE. DUNN'S MOTEL. DUNN'S MOTE. The interstate traffic was sparse, just lights moving like liquid. Charger saw the faint glow of Memphis in the west. He saw a gray car cruise by the motel slowly and then head down the service road. He turned and surveyed the lobby. The TV was blank. The coffeepot was clean and ready for morning. The clerk opened a hot-rodding magazine.

"Can't face them snakes, can you, buddy?" The guy smirked.

"That's none of your business," Charger said, coming back to the counter.

"What's private anymore?" the clerk said, with a burst of bitterness like chewing gum cracking. He set down his magazine and smoothed the cover with his palm, as if he were ironing. "Nothing's a secret. All them numbers we've got nowadays? Why, I could take your credit-card number and use it if I was of a mind to. It's all in the computers anyway. The government knows everything about everybody. It's not enough to take your taxes. They want to keep up with the news on you too. And *we* pay for their meddling. They can peep into them computers and find out anything they want to."

Charger decided to humor the guy. Somehow, he didn't want to go back upstairs just yet. "If they're that good, they could find my daddy," he said.

"Is he on the FBI list?" The clerk seemed impressed.

Charger shrugged. "No, he took a wrong turn and he just kept going."

"If they want to find him, they'll get him. They've got their ways. They come in here on stakeouts all the time. Them black helicopters that come over? They have computers right on board that plug into a global network."

"Bullshit," Charger said. *"Irk, irk,"* he muttered to himself.

The clerk looked angry, ready to pounce at him. He had a belligerent gleam in his eye. Then he seemed to steady himself. "Matter of fact, right before you came in, I checked in an escaped convict," he said in a superior tone. "He's in the room right next to you."

Charger felt his stomach flip. But he was on to the guy, he thought. He was a fruitcake. More bullshit, Charger decided. He stared the guy in the eye—magnified by the bottle-bottom glasses—until the clerk looked away. "If he's in his room, he won't hurt nobody," Charger said. "He's probably tired. He probably couldn't get a wink of sleep in jail."

The clerk opened a newspaper. "Look at this picture. That's him."

The photograph showed a dark-haired guy with a receding hairline who wore a prison work shirt and had a serial number on his chest. The headline read PRISON ESCAPEE SOUGHT IN THREE STATES.

"He signed his name 'Harry Martin' when he checked in," the clerk said. "But the guy in the newspaper is named Arthur Shemell. Look." He punched the newspaper with his finger. "Didn't fool me!"

Charger felt his confidence ebb a little. "Well, call the police, then."

"Oh, I don't want to bother them tonight. I've had them

out here on so many cases—drug busts and kidnappings. Sometimes they don't appreciate my efforts. I don't owe them any favors." The clerk shook the newspaper.

"I know what you mean," Charger said. "Been there, done that."

"Dittos."

"Been there, done that," repeated Charger, testing the sound.

The clerk folded the newspaper to display the escapee's picture. "I don't believe he's Harry Martin *or* Arthur She-mell. He's the spittin' image of Clarence Smith, this guy back in high school I used to know. He used to sneak into the girls' locker room and steal their basketball bloomers. He had one eyebrow that went all the way across. Them's the guys to watch out for. And their ears stick out too far. His whole family was like that, and they were *all* bad; one time the big-daddy busted out of the house with a hatchet and swung it at his uncle's wife's daddy—for no good reason. He split his head right open like a watermelon. That happened half a mile from my house—in 1938."

The clerk rattled the newspaper in Charger's face so quickly that Charger jumped. The guy's own ears were airplane wings, he thought.

"I hear you, buddy," Charger said, trying to calm him. He wasn't afraid of any escaped convict, but the nut behind the counter was a different story. Charger drummed his fingers loudly on the counter. I can do this, he thought.

"Well, if we've got an escaped convict here, we better get the cops on him," Charger said. "Or do you think that would be government interference? Maybe everybody should just go free. Is he a serial killer or what?"

"Bank robber, gas-station holdup, attacked his brother with a jigsaw, stole a thousand dollars from his sister—her trousseau money. Bad, bad, bad."

Charger breathed once and talked fast. He said, "Hey man, I'm busy. I've got a girl upstairs about to pee in her pants if I don't get up there. But it looks like we need to call the law on this old pal of yours, whatever his name is." Charger grabbed the portable telephone and dialed 911. Tiffany's scarf fell to the floor.

"You don't need to do that," the clerk said, reaching across the counter.

"Hey," Charger said. "No problem." He trotted a few steps out of reach.

Nine-one-one answered. Charger said, "This is the night clerk at Dunn's Motel off of exit forty-eight." He made his voice low and conspiratorial. "We've just checked in that escaped convict that was in the paper. He's your guy, folks. Come on out to our crummy little motel next to the BP off exit forty-eight. I'll hold him for you." He punched the OFF button and returned the phone to the counter with a bang. "It's all yours, buddy. Now I'm going to go get some sleep. Thanks for the opportunity to serve." He picked up the scarf.

The clerk was trembling. "Stay here with me till the cops get here," he said. "Please."

Charger rolled his eyes. "Sorry, buddy. Gotta get back to my Nellie-babe." At the door he said, "So long. If he's really a convict, they'll get him. Be sure to tell about them basket-ball bloomers."

The clerk stared, bug-eyed.

The blue scarf flying from his fist, Charger ran up the con-crete steps like a fugitive. He imagined blue lights flashing in the distance. He heard rain spatters on the asphalt. But he felt a spurt of elation. He plunged into the room and bolted the door.

"What's going on?" Tiffany asked. She was standing in the

bathroom doorway, holding a towel around her. "I was afraid something had happened to you."

"It's O.K. I got your scarf."

Tiffany retreated into the bathroom. Charger turned out the lamp by the chair and then the lamp by the bed. He heard water running in the shower. The bathroom door was ajar, and the crack of light was like a beam from a projection booth. He watched out the window from behind the edge of the drapes. Several minutes passed. Then a cruiser floated in quietly, its roof light making blue patterns on the concrete-block wall in front. Only one cop was in the car. The cop got out slowly, adjusting his heavy belt. Charger could see him and the night clerk in the doorway of the lobby. Their arm gestures seemed to suggest that the two were acquaintances. The cop shook his head knowingly, as though listening to a speeder's excuses. Finally, he waved and returned to his cruiser. The night clerk rolled up the newspaper and beat his leg. Charger kept looking, as if something more were supposed to happen.

"Is there some kind of trouble down there?" Tiffany said, moving toward him. She was wrapped in towels. By now the cruiser was gone, and the clerk had retreated into his back room.

"I'll be ready in a minute," Charger said, his voice muffled by the drape.

All he wanted was to get to Texas, Charger thought, to see those skies. He glanced up into the light-shimmering drizzle. If he got an early start on what his father had gone to see, maybe he would not mind what was to come later. It would be a way to fool destiny. "My little donkey and me," he murmured, turning and reaching for her.

ABOUT THE AUTHOR

BOBBIE ANN MASON is the author of *Shiloh and Other Stories,* which won the PEN/Hemingway Award, *Feather Crowns,* which won the Southern Book Award and was a finalist for the National Book Critics Circle Award, and the bestselling novel *In Country.* Her memoir, *Clear Springs,* was one of 210three finalists for the Pulitzer Prize. Her short fiction has appeared in *The New Yorker, The Atlantic, DoubleTake, Harper's, The Paris Review,* and elsewhere, and has received two O. Henry Awards and two Pushcart Prizes.

ABOUT THE TYPE

This book was set in Galliard, a typeface designed
by Matthew Carter for the Merganthaler Lino-
type Company in 1978. Galliard is based on the
sixteenth-century typefaces of Robert Granjon.